ALL WALLS COLLAPSE

ALL WALLS COLLAPSE

Stories of Separation

EDITED BY SARAH CLEAVE &
WILL FORRESTER

First published in Great Britain in 2022 by Comma Press.

www.commapress.co.uk

'These Days' by Geetanjali Shree was first published in Hindi as 'Aajkal' by Rajkamal Publishers (2012).

A CIP catalogue record of this book is available from the British Library.

ISBN: 1912697572
ISBN-13: 9781912697571

This book is produced in collaboration with English PEN, in celebration of ten years of its's PEN Translates programme.

FREEDOM
TO **WRITE**
FREEDOM
TO **READ**

The publisher gratefully acknowledges assistance from Arts Council England.

Supported by
ARTS COUNCIL
ENGLAND

Contents

CONTENTS

Foreword

IN THIS AGE OF nationalisms and the construction of walls that divide, it is vital to imagine the possibility of other approaches. I have written elsewhere about the artifice – and even the absurdity – of the idea of the national passport, and the possibility of a global citizenship that would introduce greater porousness into the constructions that divide us.

Restlessness and movement are inherent in the human condition. The building of walls and other means of separation will not stop us. Nowhere is this starker than in the efforts of migrants to cross the English Channel, despite the latest egregious threat of being banished to Rwanda.

Walls also permeate our writing and our literature. Stories have always been written about movement, about the experiences of separation and segregation, about the desire to remove or cross barriers. Arguments for the free movement of people go hand in hand with ideas about the free movement of words and ideas. English PEN has been working to support this movement for more than a century, and it is an idea that shapes the opening words of the PEN Charter: 'Literature knows no frontiers and must remain common currency among people.'

The unfettered transmission of words and ideas is a fundamental tenet of the right of free expression. It is the font from which all other rights spring – including those rights that are thwarted by walls of separation and the fences that intern and close national borders.

Writing plays a vital role in recording the harms imposed by borders and barriers. It also has a role to play in connecting readers and writers across national and linguistic boundaries. It fosters the possibility of change, allowing us to imagine a different age, one in which rights may be respected and nationalisms curtailed. Walls may leave a mark on literature, but literature too may leave its imprint on our walls.

We know the harms that come with the erection of fences that separate families, or block a route that may offer sanctuary. We know the harms that are wrought when borders are moved against the law, in pursuit of expansion or imperial desire. We know the harms that are brought by acts of imprisonment by reason not of what someone has done, but who they happen to be.

This book offers stories about those harms. Yet it also offers hope: about the commonalities that connect us across partitions; about resistance to separation and nationalism; about tolerance and unity; and for a world in which we can imagine the collapse of the walls erected to divide us, and the recognition of a common humanity. In this way, literature offers hope, of a place with no frontiers.

Philippe Sands
Rome, May 2022

Introduction

WALLS AND STORIES AREN'T natural bedfellows. Walls, fences, barriers, borders – physically built or constructed by non-physical means – keep in or out, separate, delineate, segregate. Stories are our common currency, the means by which we connect and share, often across national, linguistic and other intersecting lines. Boiled down in this way, walls and stories fundamentally disagree in their outlooks on the world. And so it makes sense that the history of writing about walls is a history of condemning them, smuggling across them, digging under or climbing over them, revealing their gaps and flaws and crumbling fault-lines, caring about the lives that they affect.

The walls in which the contributors to this collection are interested are not walls that shelter, or support ceilings, or hold back the elements. They are not 'neutral' walls. They are border barriers, the fences of internment and refugee camps, screens that block sight of marginalised communities, walls that manifest as the constant, silent and invisible segregation of peoples.

All Walls Collapse: Stories of Separation marks ten years of PEN Translates, English PEN's award for international literature that has made possible the publication of 300 books translated from 90 languages, including 12 books published by Comma Press. It was developed as part of English PEN's centenary in 2021, which explored 100 years of supporting the free movement of words and ideas across national and linguistic borders, and of advocating for writers at risk around the world – including those put between the walls of prison cells for no other reason than their act of writing. When Comma Press and English PEN looked at our shared values and missions, at the urgent global issues of this particular moment in history, and at the ideas underpinning the translation of literature, we arrived at the concept of the wall – the structures that try to separate us along cultural, national, ethnic, linguistic and a whole gamut of intersecting lines – as the theme for this collection.

An indictment of our time, and of our recent global histories, is that there were always going to be more walls than could be included in this book. We could have commissioned stories on the Peace Lines of Belfast, on the segregating town planning of Johannesburg, on the Great Firewall of China, on the Michalovce wall that ghettoises Roma communities in Slovakia, and on the regressive barriers that lie between most nation states and even international unions. And we hope that *All Walls Collapse* can be a part of efforts to amplify such stories of resistance to separation; stories always exist, and our obligation as publishers, editors, platforms and readers is to give them air when their authors want it, in responsible, non-extractive and ethical ways.

The walls we were able to include in this collection represent a wide breadth of geography, language, form, history and perspective. The writers we commissioned all have an interest in the themes of community, social history, the everyday lives of people and art as resistance, and in the short story form. They were given just one prompt – a specific wall, fence or border – and were invited to write a piece of short fiction that responded to this prompt in any way, in any style or genre, from any point in time. Some of the translators commissioned to craft these stories into English have worked for years with their writers; others are working together for the first time. Their acts of translation are in themselves forms of border-crossing, traversing linguistic barriers that, in some of the contexts in this anthology, are a part of wider conflict or segregation. What is remarkable is that, whilst these stories are unique to their geographic, political and language contexts, they reveal connection across time and space and culture in ways that point to the universal condition of separation and the universal currency of literature.

In 'This Side of the Wall', translated from the Spanish by Rosalind Harvey, Juan Pablo Villalobos charts the personal story of a man growing up in Mexico, with his cousins over on the 'other side' in the US. From the narrator's childhood in the 1980s, when his father erects a perimeter wall around their hurriedly built family house, through to his time in Tijuana in 1998, when fences run down into the sea, and to Donald Trump's election in 2016, Villalobos charts the ways in which border walls inflect lives and relationships as they are built, extended, and rebuilt. Kyung-Sook Shin explores another national border in 'What the Cat Passed On', translated from the Korean by Anton Hur: the demilitarized zone (DMZ) between North and South Korea. It's a border notoriously impervious to humans, but not to cats, and not to yearning, as the feline narrator and the child with whom he forges a bond discover in this singularly poignant story.

Border walls have a long history of not only separating states, but of being erected in and between disputed and occupied territories. In 'Brandy Sour' – Constantia Soteriou's contribution, translated from the Greek by Lina Protopapa – a hotel on Cyprus' Green Line bears witness to a century of conflict and unity across division. Structured around nine drinks, and the people who consume them in and around the hotel, 'Brandy Sour' moves across generations and communities to reveal small, intimate, personal moments that shape wider histories. Zahra El Hasnaoui Ahmed's 'Collateral Damage', translated from Saharawi Spanish by Dorothy Odartey-Wellington, is another piece of historic scope. A story that combines historical exposition and personal reflection, it explores the longest but perhaps least-known of the walls in this collection: the Western Sahara Wall, 1,700 miles of sand berms, barbed wire and stone structures, extended six times over the last 40 years, separating Moroccan-controlled areas in Western Sahara from territory controlled by the Saharawi Arab Democratic Republic, touching the borders of Morocco and Mauritania. El Hasnaoui Ahmed interrogates the actions of colonial and postcolonial governments in the region, and how they have touched the lives of ordinary Saharawi people – often in horrific ways – as the berms have grown and grown.

Maya Abu Al-Hayat's 'The Gap', translated from the Arabic by Yasmine Seale, looks at a concrete wall referenced by El Hasnaoui Ahmed: the West Bank Barrier Wall in Israel and the Occupied Palestinian Territories. The story's central character surveys the wall being built in his village with an adopted dog (cats, dogs and other animals appear throughout *All Walls Collapse*, traversing the barriers erected by humans), convinced he will find a gap in it, because, 'wherever there is a wall, there must be a gap.' Al-Hayat reveals the personal, familial and relationship struggles that come from walls – their erection and efforts to pass through them.

A wall might take the form of a single line that separates, but walls and fences and barriers might also come together to enclose, keeping people in or out on all fronts. It is the fences that enclose Uyghur communities in the Xinjiang internment camps that Muyesser Abdul'ehed Hendan explores in 'Reunited', translated from the Uyghur by Munawwar

Abdulla. In this story, we find a young boy wandering in the frozen north of the province, searching for his parents. A half-eaten apple in the snow prompts memories and reflections on how he has arrived in this bitter landscape. It is a story of heartrending beauty and horror, revealing the lines drawn between communities, between languages, and in the physical perimeters of internment camps. In 'Between Two Infernos', translated from the Rohingya by Hla Hla Win, Rezuwan Khan describes the enclosed life of Rohingya refugees in Kutapalong in Cox's Bazar, Bangladesh – the largest refugee camp in the world. It is an unflinching rendering of the horrors of Kutapalong, and a deeply personal story of how its fences debar joy – hemming in the festivities of marriage – and claim lives – preventing escape when fires break out. Khan's invocation of the sea as a barrier to refuge also speaks to a devastatingly commonplace image of migrancy: boats, rafts and individuals risking seas and oceans in pursuit of safety, not least across the Mediterranean and the English Channel.

In 2015, many of the 150,000 refugees in makeshift camps in Hungary had made the perilous crossing of the Mediterranean through the Aegean Sea when Viktor Orbán embarked on building the Hungary border barrier on the country's borders with Serbia and Croatia. It is a moment that Krisztina Tóth explores in 'The Fence', translated by Peter Sherwood, where a man and (another) dog become gravely unwell, and their conditions precipitate an unfolding of events that connect 2015 with the 1956 Revolution, and the contemporary border with the Iron Curtain. It is a story that reveals how decades-long cycles of separation, enclosure and suppression connect, and how they can forge suppressed trauma and jarring personal views. 'Mother's MacGuffin' by Larissa Boehning, translated from the German by Lyn Marven, is another piece that straddles eras, with its intergenerational snapshot of a family divided by the forces of the Cold War, and secrets that refuse to stay buried.

INTRODUCTION

These stories all share an interest in the relationships between physical walls and social, political or psychogeographical frontiers; the ways in which concrete barriers far away or from long ago can manifest in invisible, sometimes silent barriers between communities and individuals. Geetanjali Shree's 'These Days', translated from the Hindi by Daisy Rockwell, takes place nowhere near the India-Pakistan Line of Control fencing. Yet that long national border is palpable on a particular verandah of a particular house in a particular street as rumour, violence and fire threaten to tear along the line between religious groups in this extraordinary story of defiant friendship and quiet resistance. Rio de Janeiro's Wall of Shame – the barriers erected ahead of the 2016 Olympic Games to hide the city's favelas from sight – again finds multiple forms in Paulo Scott's 'Translucency', translated from the Portuguese by Daniel Hahn: a phone screen, a camera lens, the military police. It is a story that gets at the ways in which walls, physical and conceptual, are both symptoms of a ghettoised society and perpetuating causes of further separation; it is a story of how class, race and gender intersect; it is a story, also, of defiant hope.

The 11 pieces in *All Walls Collapse: Stories of Separation* are united not just in theme, but in form. The short story is a rather slippery thing: it makes critics say variously that it is suited to modern life and time-poor readers, or that it demands slow, immersed, careful engagement; it is a writer's way into the novel, maybe, or perhaps it is the form for the novelist who has finally got their story down to its singular utterance; it is a fragment of an unwritten whole, or a whole with unwritten fragments. The pieces in this anthology do with the short story what is needed, stretching its canvas or shrinking it to chronicle, challenge and condemn the divisive force of walls – sometimes over a century, sometimes over just a few minutes – with all the beauty and truth that the form accommodates.

INTRODUCTION

Read together, the stories in this collection allow us to see — across time, culture and space — the ways in which the condition of separation is a shared condition, but one that constellates differently across the world. You will read descriptions of the beauty of nature, the trauma of intergenerational loss, the yearning for movement, the hope of resistance, and the bonds of family throughout this collection, but each will be a natural environment that could be nowhere other than where it is, a loss collective to a particular community, a specific kind of yearning, a particular hope, a unique conception of family. What *All Walls Collapse* reveals, like all translated literature, is the ways in which stories are at once universal and unique.

Walls and stories might not be natural bedfellows, but that is because the expansive spirit of the latter will always challenge the circumscriptive spirit of the former. Stories can chronicle the effects of walls, which is why this book's subtitle is *Stories of Separation*. But they can also be a part of tearing them down, and that's why we decided that its title would be, defiantly, *All Walls Collapse*.

Will Forrester, London
& Sarah Cleave, Manchester,
May 2022

Translucency

Paulo Scott

Translated from the Portuguese by Daniel Hahn

AT THIS EXACT MOMENT, my future fellow doctoral student in Psychology at the Fluminense Federal University, who will be my partner in establishing the foundation to care for children aged up to six, a part of the group of children who lost their parents in the Second Great Invasion, and who will also become my best friend, is walking out of her home in the Maré Complex, here in Rio de Janeiro's Northern Zone, on her way to the panel of examiners before whom she will be defending her master's thesis in Psychology at the Federal University of Rio de Janeiro. The panel will meet in a room in one of the buildings on the regional campus that is immediately next to Maré, on Fundão Island. To reach one of the three access points to the island, you need only cross the expressway called the Red Line. She is carrying her rucksack containing the printed copy of her dissertation, the pencil case with pencils and pens, her ID card, her public transport card, a sliced white-bread sandwich with butter and cheese, a twenty-real note and a box of throat lozenges. In the back pocket of her trousers, she has her phone, its acrylic screen all scraped and scratched from having been dropped so frequently on the floor. She's holding the second-hand Canon EOS Rebel T100, with the EF75-300mm lens, also second-hand, which her mother gave her when she turned fifteen. She always has the camera with her, she uses it to record the people she encounters when wandering the streets of her neighbourhood. The camera has been with her for eleven years and in that time it has provided good images of people occupying the locations in that place. She no longer remembers the exact date on which she decided to take photos every day, without exception, of the people in her community, but she does remember the expression on the face of the girl slightly younger than her (she was sixteen at the time), who, on seeing the camera in her hands, came over and, totally direct, asked her to take a photo of her little daughter, who was turning two that day, so as to make the most of the beautiful new dress the girl was wearing, which had a richness to it that the lens on a cheap phone like hers would never be able to capture. My future friend took not one photo but several of the little girl in her new dress, and then she took photos of the other children who were around them celebrating the birthday joy. It was her first time taking photos of the inhabitants of Maré that weren't of her own friends or relatives. At home, there's only her and her mother, but there are plenty of uncles, aunts and cousins scattered around the Maré neighbourhoods. The next day when she walked, camera in hand, through the same area and passed some of the children she had photographed the previous afternoon, they ran over and asked her to take new photos of them. My future friend took photos of each one and enjoyed doing it. The same thing happened the next day and on those following, in that same place and others in Maré. Something else she remembers when she thinks about the time she started taking photos systematically and regularly of the people in that place is a line she read in a book of essays about photography that she found in Maré's Public Library, a line about photographs being the place where all things went that were about to disappear, things on the verge of extinction. It also said in the book that, very often, the only surviving records of geographical and architectural features, plants, animals and even groups of human beings that have disappeared from the face of the earth were images captured by tourists. Rio de Janeiro is a tourist city, and many of the photos that have been taken of the city are photos that have been taken by tourists. My future friend still has a while until her thesis defence. She isn't worried about the time. Not to be under any pressure from the time, even knowing that two and a half hours from now she will be sitting in front of professors who will assign her a grade that might determine her future plans, is lucky. The whole day has been set aside for her final academic commitment as a Psychology master's student. Which is why, without paying any attention to the time (she has a tic of checking the time every minute when she's running late, which is not the case today), nor to the WhatsApp messages sent by her acquaintances from Maré who know about her thesis defence this afternoon and, most of all, those sent by her mother asking if everything's OK, if she's all good, and telling her to take it easy because God will help and everything will work out and she will be awarded the degree of Master of Psychology for which she has striven so hard, getting the top grade, she decides to take some photos of the children who usually play outside the shop that one of her cousins has that repairs, sells cases for and installs screen protectors for phones and to make the most of the stop to put a new protective glass covering onto her own.

Last night when her mother got back from the house of the photographer where she's been in service for almost thirty years and drew her daughter's attention to its not being decent, when she's actually sitting in front of a panel for an academic thesis defence, for her to present herself with such an ill-treated phone, with its screen all destroyed like that, about how it's not very elegant, how it's not polite, my future friend tried to change the subject. Her mother insisted, asking hadn't she said she'd have to keep track of the time of her presentation and of her answers to the questions they would put to her, so wouldn't the device have to be left on the table visible while she talked? My future friend answered yes. Then her mother shook her head at the entirely unpresentable state of her daughter's phone and said no more about it. In the shop, my future friend's cousin tells her that the phone screen is so badly destroyed that it really wouldn't make any difference if she installed a glass protector or not, that it'll still look like the phone of someone just back from the war, and, using the didactic tone she usually reserves for her customers, explains that the function of the glass film is to crack, break or shatter, in the place of the acrylic of the screen, when it takes the impact, and that it's not to cover up the ugliness of the device. My future friend asks her to install the protector anyway.

Acrylic is not glass, and it does not respond mechanically like glass. Acrylic is a plastic, a high-quality plastic, a mass of large molecules, or polymers, formed from a lot of small molecules, monomers, all bonded alongside one another. This fusing process is called polymerisation. In practice this is how it works: in the empty space between two sheets of glass, two sheets that are very clean and positioned in parallel to form a mould, a whitish acrylic syrup is injected and a bit of light pressure applied to make the syrup spread evenly, then a machine takes this sandwich, the two sheets of glass and the syrup between them, into a furnace at a temperature of 90 °C under a pressure of $5kg/cm^2$. It's in this calculated combination of chemical reaction and application of the laws of physics with the making of and profiting from industrial capital that one finds the magic that produces acrylic and its high transparency, a transparency that is a very good imitation of the transparency of glass.

Anyone arriving in Brazil from abroad, coming through the city of Rio de Janeiro, unless they can afford a helicopter, will come down the Red Line, that expressway that links the international airport of Rio de Janeiro with the city centre of Rio de Janeiro. In 2010, the Municipal Government of Rio de Janeiro put transparent acrylic boards along one side of the high-speed road. These enormous boards were installed within enormous metal structures, the whole enormous wall of transparent acrylic separating the expressway that is travelled by cars transporting everything, including tourists, from the Maré Complex (or the Maré Favela, as the tourists say, romantically), from the people who live here, in Maré. The Municipal Government of Rio de Janeiro called the acrylic boards acoustic barriers. Total joke of a name. Everybody knows, even the most ill-informed, when they see the wall of acrylic sheets for the first time, that they are not acoustic barriers, they are obstacles to stop certain people who apparently live in Maré from coming down in gangs to plunder the cars when it's gridlock time on the road, to stop hundreds of hawkers wandering the road to work at selling mineral water and soft drinks on hot days, selling cassava starch biscuits in the evenings to those heading out of the city, to stop the tourists with their photographic equipment from feeling like they're being exposed to a Rio de Janeiro that perhaps they would rather not face quite so close-up.

My future friend comes out of her relative's shop with her phone covered in that glass film, intended to beautify the phone that can no longer be beautified, and her plan now is to stroll over to the stop for the bus that will take her to another stop, where she will take another bus, which goes to the campus on Fundão. Like they say in Maré: Maré and Fundão, so near and yet so far. She takes a few photos of two girls. She stopped to take their picture because she recognised them, they are the girls who, months earlier, posed for her alongside the acrylic panels, which the Municipal Government of Rio de Janeiro calls acoustic barriers, the panels that were given stickers for the Olympics that happened months earlier. At the time, my future friend, like so many other people who live in Rio de Janeiro, whether in the rich parts or in the parts where the urban space is systematically subjected to constant violence from the forces of state security, from police militias and from the drug dealers, read in the local press: *With just four weeks to go till the start of the Rio Olympics, the Municipality has finished putting coloured stickers on the acrylic sheets that run down the side of the Red Line, down which every delegation of athletes due to compete in the most important sporting event on the planet will pass. Behind this wall is the Maré Complex, a group of favelas, one of the largest and most violent communities in the state capital. According to a statement from the Secretary of Tourism, the sole function of the stickers that they have put on the barrier is to make the city beautiful, with no intention of hiding the favela from the eyes of the athletes and visitors arriving in Rio de Janeiro.* The girls say goodbye, my future friend continues on her way down one of the neighbourhood's main roads. A few dozen metres further on, she turns a corner and spots some soldiers from the army, soldiers who were deployed to the region to maintain order in the city during the Olympic games then stayed, assaulting four teenagers. She takes out her camera and starts snapping photos and moves closer. When she is very near, she puts the camera in her rucksack, shouts at the soldiers to stop this violence at once and starts filming on her phone. She keeps moving towards the soldiers warily until suddenly she feels a strong blow to her hand, a blow that makes her drop her phone on the ground. It's an officer from the military police, nearly two metres tall, who's just appeared from who knows where. And behind him, three more. She just looks at her phone on the ground, no way of knowing whether the protective glass broke or not, while one of the three who have arrived grabs her rucksack and yanks it off her shoulder, opens it, and takes out and then throws onto the floor the printed copy of her dissertation, the pencil case with pencils and pens, the wallet with her documents and the twenty-real note, the sliced white-bread sandwich with butter and cheese, the box of throat lozenges. When he pulls out the camera, he asks what a jumped-up slum-rat like her is doing with a professional camera. My future friend says it's not a professional camera, it's an old camera that's not really worth much. The military police officer asks if it's stolen. She says no. He asks for the receipt for the camera. She says she has it at home. The officer says she's lying, that he's going to confiscate the camera. She doesn't reply, stops staring straight at him, tears starting to run down her face. One of the other three, not the one who struck her hand with the blow that made her drop the phone, takes the camera from his comrade's hand, pulls out the memory card and checks that no images have been recorded in any internal memory of the device, puts the memory card in his pocket, hands her the camera, takes the rucksack from the hand of the one who threw her objects onto the ground, bends down, picks up the strewn objects, puts them back into the rucksack, hands her the rucksack, takes the phone, its glass cracked, returns it to her and instructs her to erase what she's been filming. My future friend obeys. The police officer takes the phone from her to check that the file really has been erased. She says they can't do what they're doing to her. The officer returns the phone and says that, unlike his three colleagues, he knows exactly who she is. She repeats that they can't do what they're doing to her. The officer tells her not to push her luck and to go back to where she came from. The boys she tried to help are now immobilised on the ground.

I am the teenager who, at that moment, filmed and is still filming in secret everything that happened to my future friend and is still happening to the teenagers who remain immobilised on the ground, suffering violence from the soldiers from the Brazilian Army, now with the added participation of the violence of the four officers from the Rio de Janeiro state military police. I will shortly be posting the videos I am recording onto an online video platform and what happened to my future fellow doctoral student in Psychology at the Fluminense Federal University, my future partner in the establishing of the foundation to care for children aged up to six, a part of the group of children who lost their parents and relatives in the Second Great Invasion, my future best friend, and what happened to the three teenagers, one of whom was my age, will become public and will have national repercussions.

The repercussions of the video I'm now filming of the military police officer coming up behind my future friend and suddenly striking her wrist hard and launching her phone onto the ground, and then also throwing onto the ground the things that were inside her rucksack, will be the biggest of all, much bigger than the cut in which the other military police officer gathers her things up again. The videos will be the start of the worsening of relations between my future friend and the Rio de Janeiro state military police, which, one day (from her never staying silent again and just accepting that she had to be humiliated again, going back the way she'd come, arriving ten minutes late at the panel for assessing her thesis on childhood in Maré and the self-esteem projected in the images she had photographed as a possibility of different narratives and different political expectations, the panel that would award her a top grade) will lead to a series of arrests until, one critical day, she will react more aggressively, in self-defence (the judge on the case did not accept the proposition of legitimate defence, legitimate defence being something that only people with light skin, in good financial circumstances, living in the richer areas of the city of Rio de Janeiro could plead), causing, with the point of one of her pens, a serious injury to the eye of a military police officer who humiliated her in front of the people of her community. For this desperate act, she will be sentenced to six years' imprisonment.

After the police's ordering her to go back the way she had come, my future friend walks towards the acrylic wall separating the Red Line from Maré, sits on a concrete bench opposite a public football pitch and there she stays, in a state of shock, for several long minutes. By chance, an acquaintance of hers, who knows she is due to be defending her dissertation pretty soon, sees her from a distance and comes over to ask if she isn't going to her academic appointment, and my future friend comes back to her senses, walks over to one of the boards in which holes have been made to allow people to get through to sell mineral water and soft drinks on the hot days, cassava starch biscuits in the evenings, and goes through. She crosses the Red Line paying little attention to the cars, she walks to one of the access bridges to the island, enters the campus and heads for the building with the room where the professors are already waiting for her.

My future friend would not end up getting imprisoned for six years, but she will spend a good while in detention. It won't be until the year after her release that she goes back to taking photos and starts to practice psychology. One day she will decide to go back to studying. That will be when I have the good fortune of, in one of those coincidences in life you can't explain, sharing two courses with her.

One day my future friend will tell me that she's happy to know that when she types Maré Complex into Google Images what she finds are many more beautiful photos taken by people in the community than photos of violence, photos of soldiers occupying our area, or photos taken from the other side of the acrylic panels, probably by tourists. I will reply that when I looked at the acrylic wall from the perspective of our community I imagined the cars travelling down the Red Line as agitated animals trapped in an enormous cage. And she will laugh. That will be after the Second Great Invasion of Brazil, the Second Great Invasion that is not the subject of this story, the subject of this story beginning and ending with the concept of acrylic.

A human skull struck by something capable of breaking its structure, such as, for example, a rubber bullet fired at short range, or a real bullet fired at a greater distance, can be reconstructed with acrylic.

Acrylic is also used in tactical shields, known as riot shields, which are used by the Rio de Janeiro state military police.

Acrylic is used in the screens of smartphones, smartphones that photograph and film with much greater ease of handling than a regular camera or video camera.

Acrylic can be scratched.

Last year, they brought an acrylic to market that regenerates itself after it gets scratched, scraped, burned.

When it burns, acrylic does not emit smoke, its burning being like the burning of a hard wood.

In a line of poetry, acrylic can be a metaphor for dreaming and it can be many other things.

One day my future friend will tell me, though using other words, that people cannot be acrylic syrup injected into glass moulds. On another day, when I am not expecting it, she will tell me that her camera is still the best company she has and that I'm not to be jealous, that I'm the person who has most helped her not to give up.

We go on remaking ourselves, every day.

These Days

Geetanjali Shree

Translated from the Hindi by Daisy Rockwell

EVERY NIGHT I COME out and sit on the verandah for a while. Like I'm playing a role. My desire to sleep abandons me, running off to join the distant din that assails my ears and feeds my fantasy that the mob is on its way.

But so what if I do fall asleep? I know it'll make no difference to me, though I'm ashamed to admit it.

And I've been feeling plenty of shame, these days. My eyes keep filling with tears. Perhaps I'm growing old – they say our defences grow weak with age. Our lacrimal glands squeeze out so many tears that they come to resemble a municipal tap: dry whenever you go to turn it on, but when you haven't so much as touched it, water bursts forth, *fwoosh,* striking up a wilful *drip drip drip.* Things are so bad that I avoid looking in the mirror for fear I'll burst into tears when I recall my erstwhile beard and moustache; even when I'm nowhere near a mirror my tear ducts start acting up!

My face has completely changed since shaving off my facial hair, but I'm not afraid – why should I be? Everyone knows I've come to stay here, these days. I'm here; he's not. I leave the door open on purpose and sit about so the neighbours can see me clearly, especially early in the day when Kalua comes from his quarters with the puja aarti and I ostentatiously take part in a morning Hindu prayer, after which I ask, like I always did in the past, for a mind-blowingly strong cup of tea, following which I mosey out onto the verandah, as if to say, See? Whoever's out there, take a look. Recognise me? I'm right here. No one else. Calm down, he's not here.

Actually, forget calm; it's downright deserted around here these days. If you see anyone, it's when curfew is relaxed for a few hours in the morning: a middle-aged housewife carrying groceries in a thin bag, or a servant on a bicycle with a bucket of milk dangling from the handlebars. The bucket may clank, but no song springs from the lips of the servant, *keh do na keh do na, you are my soniya – say it now, say it now, you are my darling.* The whole atmosphere is depressing. I'd been so tired of hearing that song. It'd got to the point where just hearing the first few bars made me grit my teeth, and I'd jump up and turn off the TV with a *click*, and then, as though that click was the *on* switch for the entire city, the song would start playing from all sides. But now all the singing has skulked off to hide in some burrow.

And it isn't just singing; even the passions of youth have crept away to lie low, and young women wander about fearlessly because young men no longer come out to whistle at and harass them. But they haven't just stopped coming out to whistle, they've stopped coming out at all.

The young men you see now are of a different sort. From elsewhere. *Not local*, they say. They gather at the city clock tower and form a band, then go prowling about, bouncing anti-Muslim slogans up and down on the points of their spears and tridents. Rumour has it they're cooking up something for this area now.

But my job is to sit fearlessly on the verandah. Just stay put. Everyone knows me around here. Ask anyone – my name, my religion, what have you. Take a look – recognise me? I'm not afraid.

But fear isn't a straightforward thing; it doesn't always pop up for clearly discernible reasons. It blows about madly in the breeze, and wherever it goes it's apt to invade anyone who accidentally inhales it. Like a wandering ghost that slips into a random body and then makes a child speak like an old person; it's exactly the same with fear. Even if I know I'm in no danger – what danger could there be? – fear leaps up from behind my bravado and begins to unwrap itself like a parcel; it emerges and overtakes my fearlessness and messes with my equilibrium such that, one minute, I'm a tough guy – *Hey jackals, bring it on! But be warned, you'll pay a steep price for every drop of blood you shed* – and then the next minute, here am I, tail between my legs, a mouse, searching through the shrubbery for a hidey-hole.

I get up and turn on all the verandah's lights. (Weak lighting at night could create the illusion that I want to hide; that I'm the wrong guy, the one they will not spare. I am fully illuminated where I sit: See? I am visible, fearless – the right guy.)

Tomorrow is Holi's eve. Tomorrow the Holika bonfire burns and people will gather around and sing songs and roast ears of green barley and wheat.

When I was a child, everyone used to look forward to the bonfire with great excitement. The whole process of gathering wood started days before. Everywhere you looked, there were piles at the ready. Ma would smear us with a special paste that she would then rub off, removing all the dirt from our bodies with it; this mixture she'd gather in a pot to be thrown into the bonfire, to burn away all badness and filth. It was our day to get thoroughly clean, and whoop it up. We aren't Westerners, so we have no need to tremble for centuries, oppressed by the burden of original sin. We are Eastern: Poof! And the dirt is gone. Colour everywhere, high jinks in everything, a holiday in every hoopla.

The girls and boys at university also adored bonfire day. There was dancing, flirting and romance, and in every flame and every flounce, an anticipation of what mischief the Holi colours would bring on the morrow when they showered us with love.

But has something changed?

Yes, something has changed.

These days, it doesn't seem like wood being gathered is necessarily for the Holika bonfire. It could be for any bonfire. Fire is fire, after all, and hearts are so dry and brittle, it doesn't take long to set them ablaze. And then there's no telling how far the fires will spread, whether they come from the Holika blaze, or the blazing city, or the whole world on fire.

So everyone's in a constant state of vigilance and when the holiday draws near, warnings fly about like shrapnel.

I begin to feel anxious; that I'll forget to sleep. Today, Kalua was saying he too had been interrogated: When is that guy coming home? Is this guy staying here these days? This guy shouldn't be staying here. That other one isn't here, so where is he?

I should be reassured by this. It means I've been recognised, and everyone knows I'm sleeping here and they're concerned about me too. Or... I'm not sleeping, and they're concerned about me staying here!

But for some reason I feel agitated. All eyes are upon me. I'm not in the habit of occupying centre stage. I'm an ordinary citizen; I want to keep peacefully to my own little corner. How have I got caught in the spotlight? But catch me it has, and how strongly it shines: I feel stunned. Nervous. I itch to crawl, like a worm, into a deep, dark crack. But I'm afraid the lights will follow me and I'll flee the crack too – and where will I hide then? And so I sit, out in the open, a tiger face my mask, my cowardly jackal heart hidden within.

But yes, this is also what I fear: I'm protected. I sit here on the verandah, out in the open, like an announcement – Look, it's me! Not him. And I have a right to such protection, after all.

I sit here on the verandah, feeling in every pore of my being as though the buildings towering around me are people, the open windows their eyes, to which I turn, begging for a reprieve: Look, over here, take note, am I trying to hide? Why would I do that – don't you recognise me? It's me, a Hindu. I've turned on all the lights and they're all ablaze so that you can see, it's me, just me, brother, cut me some slack.

The rest of the homes are in darkness, obscured.

I looked at so many houses with my friend. We searched far and wide, discussed and debated constantly, and then he went and settled on this one. Hmm... which is better, an apartment or a house? Consider security and easy maintenance! But also imagine the fun of creating a home according to your own wishes. And then we undertook a thorough investigation of the neighbourhoods. Which neighbourhood is best? This one is right next to a market. In that one over that way, there is a community divide, with a dividing wall, like a boundary. But here, everyone is educated and friendly; some professors, some doctors; Christians, Parsis; all sorts. No wall between them.

This neighbourhood turned out to be the best in every respect and my friend took out a loan and bought this house.

I recall how run down it had been. When the older generation had departed, the son, who was of the new business-oriented mindset, was inclined to tear it down and erect a multi-storey building in its place. He planned to cut down all these trees and build out to the street, all for the smallest of profits.

I gaze at the trees in the compound through the eyes of my friend.

He must have bought this home to save the trees! A red cotton tree on the side; an old, crooked branch of a jasmine plant stretching out onto the verandah; in front, a mountain ebony, a mango, a baramasi lime and a neem. Old trees, all rooted here.

What would be the point of uprooting them? My friend was also pleased that while most people must start their gardens from seeds, this house already had mature shade trees. We imagine we're adopting such trees, but they're actually adopting us.

Love flows and flowers from them, not from us.

I recall how I used to walk over here of a morning, to visit my friend.

How I used to drink tea in the lovely shade of the trees.

Or stroll barefoot on the lawn, gazing at the buds and flowers.

I'd rest my heart on a branch, or let it swing from a leaf.

I'd fly up and sit with wings outspread in the tree with the other birds and chirp along with them.

I wonder, suddenly, if these trees will be spared. And so I feel anxious again. The din of the crowd starts up. It is far off but loud, like when you put in a hearing aid and a slight sound becomes deafening, the drop of a needle a bursting bomb.

And then I see it: a shadow. It thinks no one can see, but I can. It has passed by the other buildings in the neighbourhood and is walking up the street.

He's become just one more shadow cast by the trees that line the road.

Only thieves and prowlers behave like this, I think in a panic. A strange fear wells up inside me at the thought that he'll have to walk down the middle of the street beneath the municipal streetlights to the front gate in order to sneak into this house. What will I do then? He'll be completely visible – though I did turn the round lamp next to the gate off after dinner, to make it darker in front.

But instead of approaching the front gate he remains a shadow, and starts walking alongside the boundary wall, his head bobbing above it as he walks.

Where is he going? I wonder with dismay. There's only a cement enclosure in back, where the neighbourhood trash lies rotting. He walks as a shadow among shadows. If you don't look too closely, he might be the shadow of a tree, but if you pay attention, he does look like a prowler!

I begin to wonder what his plan is. But I stay rooted to the spot. My heart pounds and my body turns stiff as a block of wood. 'I hope nothing happens, I hope nothing happens,' I murmur to myself, as I sit there glued to my seat. Or do I simply believe that in these unique times, it's best to lay low; isn't that what people usually say?

I peek from the corner of my eye. The shadow has stopped at the rubbish heap. It stands by the branches of the red cotton tree that hang outside the compound and into the alleyway. The tree overspreads both sides of the wall.

The red cotton tree. The red cotton tree blossoms during Holi, in the month of Phagun. All the old leaves have already fallen. New shoots of pale green have begun at the tips of the branches. But they're so overwhelmed with abundant flowers they've almost disappeared. Nestled amongst the crimson petals are numerous black bees, giving the blossoms the appearance of flocks of red birds with black beaks perched on the branches all in a row, ruffling their feathers as if they could fly away at any moment.

Fly away at any moment, or flutter into the sky, when, just then, the shadow flies up and lands in a whirr on a branch of the red cotton tree.

A bird!

And up it jumps onto the wall, then drops down, hanging from the branch inside the compound.

A monkey!

Such is the human condition: we are skilled at taking one step forward and twenty steps back.

He hangs there as though he's come for the express purpose of dangling from the cotton tree. Amidst a cacophony of thoughts, it suddenly occurs to me that I can definitely assert that this is the first time in his life he has transformed into a monkey.

But assert to whom? And what a thing to assert!

I sit here like a bump on a log. What should I say? Should I move? Not move? I'm busy breathing in and out, as though my breath is walking on eggshells. These days, it's hard to say which is more dangerous: moving or sitting still like a bump on a log.

These days, people's minds are numb. They think it's best for things to stay right where they are; if a fire rages somewhere, so be it; if it dies down, so be it – as long as it doesn't come their way! They'll only come out of hiding once the fire has died out. They'll come out and they'll stand. They'll take a stand. Maybe. Maybe they will.

I stay put, still, as though the moment has arrived in which we're all in the hands of fate. Whatever happens happens; we're all drained of energy.

The shadow is determined to face its own fate.

Later, I will wonder what that game was that we both played – separately, alone, but in full knowledge of one another, putting on a show of unawareness. He, in the darkness of the tree; I, in the light of the verandah. He, on that side of the wall; I, on this. An alert hunter, seemingly nonchalant but inside poised to leap, and seize, perhaps.

He jumps noiselessly from the branch into the compound.

I suddenly feel demoralised. Yes, I will say, I felt demoralised, otherwise I wouldn't have just stayed sitting there as though I had no idea what's going on.

Yes, I will say, I had no idea what was going on, that's why

I stayed sitting there, weirdly deflated. The way a person grows calm when they hear the footfall of Death approaching. They prepare to die, immobile, calm.

The shadow hunkers down right where it lands. A squatting shadow leaning against the trunk of the cotton tree, resting.

We both sit motionless for what seems like an age, each in our place. Bound up in a bizarre game. Bound up in waiting. We are besieged by a quiet dread: do what you must, whatever it takes. May you find reprieve somehow.

I'm not looking, but still, I see: he stands and, for just an instant, walks within range of the light. My heart jumps. What if I lose control and turn my head that way? What if I look over there by accident while I'm doing something else? He holds his head low, as if a shiver has run down his spine. Now he shifts from the light back into the darkness. He's at the side door of the house. A snake shivers and sways before suddenly disappearing.

Shadow, wood. Bird, monkey, snake. What more will we become?

Fasten the chain, but don't bolt the door – which I haven't done – so that the door can be gently pushed ajar, and one can reach inside to unfasten the chain. Everyone will call me careless, I think, and I sit with bated breath, as if by not breathing I can ensure my future ability to breathe.

How mad we've all become.

I again begin to think about this house, as though this is the only way to forget the shadow. As though the shadow and this house are two separate entities. As though that shadow is not inside the house at this very moment.

This house will burn, too. With me in it. With him in it. Today. Now. Tomorrow. In the Holika bonfire. *Keh diya keh diya you are my soniya – I told you, yeah, I told you, yeah, you are my darling.*

Rumour or truth? But, these days, it doesn't take long for rumours to transform into truth. A rumour flies aloft;

everyone considered it simply a rumour when they heard there was a plot afoot to desecrate the 500-year-old tomb of a musician, but desecrate it they did, and thus a rumour was no longer a rumour. The musician was finished off 500 years after the fact.

Death comes only when the soul burns. Who will die when this house burns down? How long will wraiths and spirits haunt it after that?

I begin to feel heavy and numb; a corpse growing corpsier.

The shadow is in the study now, moving slowly. Slower and slower. But I still feel like I'm wearing hearing aids. Every sound is magnified. A drawer opening, closing. Papers and documents riffling. Its breathing.

When the shadow moves, the front part of its foot appears in the light. Pushing the bedroom door open just a crack, enough to draw a slice of light – a border – in the study. My only job had been to leave on the bedside lamp. I wouldn't turn it off until I went to sleep. That's what I've been doing since I came here.

Different bits of the shadow now flash intermittently into view: a hand on the wardrobe door, a foot on the carpet, a shoulder next to the switchboard. And with these flashes, items in the room also shift about. The rest is darkness. A green duffle bag drags itself out. The bag enters the study and begins filling with dribs and drabs. Fingers alight upon toiletries in the bathroom, and out they hop. The large wardrobe pushes forth hangers and they shrug off the clothing draped on them and hand it to the darkness. The key to the safe comes jangling out from beneath the mattress and the things locked there flow into a sliver of hand.

Later, I will think about how ordinary household items jumped into the duffle bag in the shadow's darkness as I sat numbly outside. They sprang to life, like in fairy tales. And the bits and bobs of the shadow would emerge from nooks and crannies to make contact with the body filling the duffle bag, as though holding an advisory meeting to discuss matters past and future.

In the meantime, on the kitchen table, the back garden vegetables that Kalua picked only just today awaken for a moment. And as is the custom with flora and fauna, they begin to spread the fragrance of the earth in which they grew, as though the one they've awaited has finally arrived. The distinct fragrances of lime, lauki, and tomato, which I would later smell in my memories, waft onto the verandah.

Out in the garish light, I sink lower into my chair. I realise helplessly that, if and when the fire comes, all these houses, painstakingly decorated over the years, will be wiped out in the blinking of an eye. Should I stay sunken? Should I do something? Should I do nothing? Safety on the one hand and danger on the other! Which should I choose? When should I stand, when should I sit, how can I know?

Later, these become the questions that best describe my mental state at the time.

Now the shadow is returning, via the same trash heap route, from the inside branch to the outside branch, from the inside earth to the outside earth, across the border wall drawn down the middle.

Oh! My chair starts. *Oh! He's going, he'll leave!* the chair gives me a push. I'm alert. I quickly mount the verandah stairs and approach the cotton tree, as if these actions are another component of the game. Me this side, him that side, both walking with measured steps.

One day, I'll ponder this as well: how did I come to be on this side, and he on that? Of the wall! Of the darkness!

We've both reached the gate: I'm in, he's out. But here the pace of the game changes. For now, I stop, and he keeps going.

As the shadow walks down the road, the green duffle bag merges with it. I stand watching the shadow, and it knows I'm watching. It continues straight ahead along the street.

No, I don't go out into the street. If I haven't yet, why would I now? Just like someone might say: I didn't catch him yet, why should I now? Or they might say, Better that way – you never know, these days, who might be carrying a concealed weapon.

The shadow's path curves with the bend of the street. And here I am, and that's the end of that. But suddenly, somewhere, someone flings a door open. We both jump, the shadow and me. Trembling like the wind. Startled as one. We spin around, fearfully; him this way, and me that; and our eyes turn, like the tick of a clock-hand, to the next second.

It is only in that one solitary moment that we stare fixedly at one another, piercing the darkness.

That sort of moment stands still forever.

Such moments don't go anywhere. Such moments roll everyone together, and wipe out everything else. Such moments are the moments that sociologists, writers, religious figures, psychologists analyse and dissect for centuries without ever getting anywhere.

Such moments render us naked, and nakedness is uncouth; once we are naked, we are left with nothing else.

I bow my head, and a feeling of anger at being trapped like this rises within me: at that Muslim friend who came here as a shadow, in order to break into his own home; at myself for playing the decoy, so that whoever saw, saw me, and no one saw him, so that he could stuff all his worldly possessions into a duffle bag and vanish, since there was a rumour afoot that the house would be set aflame with him in it, and anyway, if you burn one, you'll burn them both, and, anyway, starting such rumours amounts to the same thing as actually lighting the fire. So that's it: the street before me lies empty and behind me sit the crimson flowers of the cotton tree in rows, wings outspread, ready, either from a sense of hopelessness or of vain hope, to fly away before they wither and die.

The Gap

Maya Abu Al-Hayat

Translated from the Arabic by Yasmine Seale

THE FIRST THING TO say about Nabil, should we wish to describe him, is that he is an optimistic man – a quality all the more striking as it has just about vanished from the village of Al-Walaja, whose residents are distinguished by their ability to find a problem for every solution. Tell them you've worked out how to bring water to the fruit trees next year, and they'll poke ten holes in your plan. Say you've found a way to get the children to school safely in winter, and they'll turn winter into a battlefield. Not so Nabil – a man who, through sheer persistence, can get around any problem; he can't even remember when he last used the word problem. His solutions may falter, they may take aeons to achieve, but they always come off in the end.

You might say it's a quality passed down the generations.

His great-grandfather Salem managed to escape certain death during the Nakba, when he and the other villagers found themselves trapped in the mosque. All the men were killed except for him, as he had found an opening in the wall of the mosque's storeroom and hid there among the old rugs until it was all over. Then he ran and didn't stop until, after sixty miles, he reached the hills of Amman.

His father's brush with certain death came in the Second Intifada. His phone had rung and saved his life (or so he daily swears), just before bullets came piercing through the wall of the room he was painting in Ramallah. As the caller remains unknown to this day, he could almost swear it was a direct call from God.

Both sources, perhaps, of Nabil's sense that all would be well in the end.

When word began to spread that the wall was due to run through his village and that his house alone would lie beyond it, cut off from his land and the homes of his relatives, he saw no issue there, and he could not understand why his wife kept howling that their livelihood was ruined, their wealth gone up in smoke, their family finished. Nabil would find a way out: he was sure of it.

As soon as digging began, in 2002, Nabil set to work. He read all the reports, the surveys and assessments, studied the maps and plans, and memorised the names of all the neighbourhoods, villages and towns the wall – all 730 kilometres of it – would cut in half. He even walked the length of the Green Line, which separates the West Bank from Israeli territory, observing the construction workers as they unloaded the large blocks of cement and slowly closed off the horizon.

Every day he'd return home and record the information he had gathered in his notebook, his black box:

On the Palestinian side, the wall consists of six coils of barbed wire, followed by a deep trench, then a dirt road for the passage of patrols, then an electronic fence three metres high.

On the Israeli side, it consists of a paved road with sandy lanes on either side, barbed wire, and electronic alarms. At certain points, the barrier is as wide as 60

metres. As for the concrete wall, it is found only in
densely populated areas. It is 8 metres high.

To support his optimistic view of things, he'd present his wife
with figures: 166 houses demolished to build the wall; 49,291
metric dunams of land confiscated, most of which had been
used for agriculture. How lucky they were, he insisted, that
their house was only separated from the village and not
demolished, that their land was only cut off by the wall and
not confiscated. That as long as it was somewhere, it was
everywhere. Assuring her all the while that he would find the
gap to let him through. For wherever there is a wall, there must
be a gap.

For ten years, Nabil left his home in the morning and
returned in the evening, hunting for the gap, trying theory
after theory as to where it might be. However strong the wall,
it seemed inevitable that the climate, animals, people, even the
earth itself expanding and contracting would have forced a
crack in it. Nabil spent long hours envisioning the moment he
would slip into the gap, having made sure no one was guarding
it or watching from afar, though it was also possible, he
reasoned, that there were trap openings created by the soldiers
to ensure their control over any gaps that may exist or to test
their new weapons.

Still, he would study all options so thoroughly that none
could escape him. He even adopted a small dog that took a shine
to him on the road, but decided not to form any sort of
emotional bond with it, not even to give it a name, so as not to
become attached. He would send it ahead of him into the gap,
when he found it, and wait to see what happened. But after a
year of going back and forth in the company of the dog (his
children, unbeknown to him, had named it Biscuit), he grew so
fond of it that he could no longer think of parting. He even
built a kennel for it opposite his home and came to think of it

as his closest companion, as did his four children and even his wife, who had lost her mind when she first saw it, declaring that the cruelty of life had sent her, instead of family and land, a dog and a mad husband who spent his whole time looking for a gap.

One day it occurred to him that the gap might be at the top rather than the bottom, as he had imagined all this time, and he felt the answer was near. He found an area outside the city of Tulkarm almost empty of residents and saw no patrols in the ten days he spent observing the road. For three months he experimented with ideas for a light ladder he might carry across a long distance, and ended up assembling one from the olive tins which had lain empty since the wall was built, as the trees were now beyond reach. Inconspicuous, easy to dismount, his ladder was ready. He waited for the promised day when he would carry it in a long bag he had bought for this purpose from the market in Jenin.

He tried not to meet anyone's eye as he walked, and it was curious that no one looked in his direction either. Then he noticed that many men and women and even schoolchildren were carrying bags similar to his, and it seemed to him that they too were hiding something, but no one looked at anyone else or asked where they were going. He reached the point he had spotted, waited quarter of an hour in case someone was watching him, then he began to remove the ladder piece by piece and set it up, Lego-style, against the wall. Having scaled it, he found he was ten centimetres short of reaching the barbed wire at the top. He had not been up there a few moments when an IDF patrol showed up and arrested him immediately.

After three years, Nabil was finally released. The gap preyed on his mind throughout his detention, and for once in his life he felt there was no way out of the predicament in which he found himself. He seemed to see things for the first time as they really were, as if he had been given a new pair of eyes: he saw his house standing alone surrounded by tall cement walls, and he saw himself without work or land or family. Things dawned on him: that his children wore the same clothes they had passed between them for years. That his wife's black shoes had turned grey. That it was years since he last took his family out for falafel.

His wife sold everything they owned and found work in the neighbouring villages making pickles and cheese for one of the women's centres, and was able to milk her sheep and see to their basic needs, but it killed her to go on living in the isolated house. He thought she was bound to leave him and take their children to live in one of the surrounding villages. And that he, too, would be forced to leave the house. When at last Nabil walked out of prison, he resolved to put the gap out of his mind for good – to give up the very thought of its existence. He entered his home broken, another man entirely. At night, when the children had gone to sleep on their mattresses side by side, his wife slowly came near. This is it, he thought. She is about to leave me for good.

Instead, from under her belt, his wife pulled out the black notebook.

'I searched everywhere on this side. Now I'm sure: the gap must be on the other side. I heard Umm Muhammad say to her neighbour that her son managed to find an opening on the south side, and that dozens of people have come and gone without being caught.'

Life had drained from Nabil's eyes – and from his hands and cheeks and guts. But his wife's words revived him in an instant. He leapt out of his seat and fell on the pages of the black notebook, which was filled with names and signs and maps, only to discover that he had indeed been looking in the wrong direction. He kissed his wife's throat – a soft burble against the night's hush. In the morning the whole family went looking for the gap.

Three years later...

For the second time this week, Palestinian youths have made a breach in the wall separating Israel from the West Bank, in a protest marking 25 years since the fall of the Berlin Wall.

His face behind a mask, the activist tied a two-metre-wide section of the concrete wall to a truck. Then it pulled away. The crowd of fifty people, who had gathered by a section of the wall near Qalandiya Checkpoint, cheered as the block of wall, six metres high, came down. Israeli forces fired tear gas at the crowd, some of whom threw stones at the wall. A number of demonstrators passed through the gap they had made, holding up the Palestinian flag.

Collateral Damage

Zahra El Hasnaoui Ahmed

Translated from the Saharawi Spanish
by Dorothy Odartey-Wellington

ME LLAMO SAFIA, y soy Sahrauia. I'll say it again: I am Safia, a Saharawi woman. It sounds good, doesn't it? Because of the alliteration, maybe? But it is a death sentence. *Sush, child. Words are carried away by the Sirocco wind.*

Suke is my favourite aunt. Or was – we don't know. She disappeared years ago for introducing herself in the same way. It seems like such an innocent way of describing yourself, but since 1975 it has been a death sentence. Africa's history repeats itself; your homeland is turned into a destination with a one-way ticket.

'Shark Island, the island of death' – that could be the title of a horror film, but it is not a fiction, as the Herero and Namaqua people in Lothar Von Trotha's Shark Island concentration camp discovered. They called it Death Island. The Germans called it Shark Island. Before that, the British had called it Star Island. It had a name before that, too, but we don't know it.

It is a sad thing to go down in history for committing an ignominious act against your fellow human beings. Wait – not exactly. Because to Von Trotha, we Africans were baboons, or something like them. It was proven – scientifically! – through craniometry, they said. We belonged to a second-class race, the brachycephalic race. The Jews, too – and they were white. Just not quite. It's hard to believe that their arrogance was so cruel; that the colonists appointed themselves as dedicated do-gooders, who would save us from ourselves, from our culture, from our ignorance. The white man's burden, as Kipling said. Poor them. Or poor rich them, very rich them, with all that plundering.

That strange, jinxed bird is to blame for so much bad luck. There are two birds of ill omen for Saharawis: the crow and the barn owl. The crow, because it is black – what an obsession! – and the barn owl, because it is a devil. Demonic creatures, messengers of doom.

In 1975, a snowy owl visited us. Yes, a white owl on the coast of the desert. How exciting, right? We went to see it, but it took off, terrified, to other lands. It would have died from the heat, or from being stoned by the crowds. It wasn't even a barn owl. It was so beautiful. And to think that we desert people are supposed to be hospitable.

1975 was the happiest and saddest year of my life. It was the last Eid that we celebrated as a family, the smell of henna and incense filling every nook and cranny of the house, the fragrance of a famous imported cologne in my father's turban, new brightly coloured melhfas, delicacies ready to be served, relatives' smiles and long greetings. Our greetings go on for minutes. A simple 'hello' is rude. We ask after family, friends, neighbours. We had visitors constantly coming and going that day in 1975, mainly so that they could fulfil their obligation to ask their loved ones, their acquaintances, and the people with whom they lived for almusamaha. They apologised for any harm they may have caused, consciously or unconsciously. On that day, sorry ceased to be the hardest word.

And there was music. Fontanella Bass's 'Rescue Me' had been playing constantly in my head since my favourite brother had disappeared and left me only with memories and his love of American soul music. With thousands of other young men, he had joined the ranks of the Saharawi army, to protect us from the Moroccan military occupation. Recently, a friend's tweet reminded me of an ancient custom: Saharawi women keep the sand from the footprints of their loved ones who have gone to war. During those months, mothers, sisters, girlfriends, wives all collected footprints to keep between the tight folds of a piece of melhfa, in a hidden corner of their memories. But I couldn't, because I didn't know what was happening. Everything was done with extraordinary silence and secrecy. You didn't know what was really happening. It was a meandering playscript with no ending in sight.

It was only years later that I discovered our people, along with almost all the rest of the African continent, had been victims of ruthless okupas. They called it colonisation.

What do you do when the Industrial Revolution brings its social and economic and demographic problems? How to solve them? Easy. Like good friends, you have a get-together in Berlin and divide the African cake among yourselves with T-squares and triangles. Although there is stiff competition between you – the European powers – over who is to have the best slice, like civilized gentlemen, you reach agreements that demarcate the borders of the territory to be exploited. If you are the Belgian king, you keep a slice for yourself – a delicious slice. And then, when independence comes, you pass down the border problems to the people whose land you have taken, adding to the other problems that they have, because you have made sure that they, too, want to claim the best slice.

On 14 November 1975, a month after celebrating Eid with my family, before abandoning its colony, Spain signed the infamous Tripartite Madrid Accords with Morocco to the north and Mauritania to the south and told them to divide the territory among themselves. All very nice indeed. I take over your house under the guise of exchanging goods, and then, rather than giving it back to you and apologising for wrongfully occupying it, I leave and pass it on to another person. How quickly our neighbours learned from their bully, France! After the Second World War, it seemed the world had been taught a lesson about the worthlessness of violence, brought on by the excessive greed of another ruthless murderer. But no. The consequences of the Covid-19 pandemic could have served as another lesson, a cause for reflection. The retaining wall that we imposed upon ourselves to save lives gave the Earth a respite. Let's implement that kind of wall. But no, our foolishness knows no bounds. We will continue to be consumed by avarice until there is nothing left of us but bones, and we all disappear as a species, to the delight and relief of the others.

In May 1975, a UN mission had come to Western Sahara to gather information on how Saharawis felt about Spanish colonisation. Most of Africa had freed itself from occupation and, stirred up by the international wave of demands for all types of freedoms, we were not going to settle for anything less. A mass demonstration, organised by the Polisario Front liberation movement, was clear in its message: independence. And that is what was reported by the visiting mission. We were getting ready to celebrate the creation of our nation when we found out about the Green March. King Hassan II of Morocco, with the help of French and American intelligence experts, pulled a classic magic trick, and while in all the international news outlets they were debating if Spain would confront the ragtag horde of the Green March – even with arms, if it became necessary – the Moroccan army was invading the territory. The decision to 'sell' the territory to its two neighbours had been agreed upon in European meeting rooms, beyond the seas, long before. According to the secret version of the agreement, Spain would safeguard its economic, public, and private interests in exchange for the illegal transfer.

When I studied the French Revolution, I adopted its slogan, because liberty, equality and fraternity reflected our best qualities, our defeat of demeaning injustice – because it summed up my objective in life. (I am afraid I am a pure product of colonisation: my cultural references are practically all Western.) Now that I am old, I have discovered that I am racialised and that I am an other. What concepts are behind those terms? Who invented this issue of race? It is as stupid as classifying people according to the colour of their eyes. But, of course, if I don't say you are black, brown, definitely non-white, and therefore an inferior being, I don't have much of a justification for enslaving or colonising you.

We Saharawis had the audacity to stand in the way of other people's interests: mostly Western people, but also other Africans. After he ascended the throne, Hassan II suffered several coups d'état. He needed to engage his people in something else – something that didn't include overthrowing the monarchy because of social discontent. He rallied his people behind him in pursuit of a common goal: jingoistic nationalism. We know that when we are overwhelmed by social and economic problems the number of nationalist parties with extremist tendencies goes up. We blame what is happening on the other, and yet are not quite sure who, because it is easier than reflecting and finding solutions. Hassan II's strategy was to dust off the wildly ostentatious map that the nationalist Istiqlal Party had designed, which included Western Sahara, Mauritania, part of Algeria and part of Mali. It would be difficult to reconquer Al-Andalus to the north, so they opted to go south. They would start with Western Sahara, claiming that they had sovereignty over the territory before colonisation, a theory that would be discounted by history and the 1975 ruling of the International Court of Justice. That didn't matter; it worked. Some 300,000 Moroccans heeded the call of His Majesty.

The images of the Green March are burned into my retinas: those loud, hopeful citizens carrying the US flag and the Qur'an, trying to cross the border between Western Sahara and Morocco. They thought they could find the solutions to their problems there. How gullible they were! Since then, the Moroccan monarchy has become one of the richest in the world. The new King has eliminated the biggest threat to his crown, coup attempts by the generals, by handing over a large portion of Western Sahara's natural resources to them. Perfect. Two birds with one stone. Meanwhile, Moroccan people are sacrificing their lives between oceans and barricades as they try to reach European soil.

We first settled in provisional camps deep in the desert, far away from the cities under military occupation. We didn't have a Saharawi army; our few soldiers were from the Spanish forces. It was going to be a temporary settlement, we thought. The exodus was not easy. We did not have the means to take care of all the people fleeing. In cars, in trucks, on foot, people were arriving from all over the territory. After we managed to cobble together our camp, safe from the tanks, the metal birds arrived, spitting napalm and phosphorous. Unlike in Vietnam, there were no photojournalists in the Sahara, and no pictures of our mutilated children travelled around the world. We sought refuge with our other neighbour, who generously let us in.

We realised that the UN was not going to do anything to bring decolonisation to fruition, nor stop the folly of a new colonisation. And so the war of liberation began. On 27 February 1976, the Saharawi Arab Democratic Republic was proclaimed. We urgently needed to organise ourselves – on the military front, yes, but also in the areas of health, education and logistics. Our war was a war of attrition. Morocco had its huge army, but that meant it had to spend millions of dollars each day, something the King wouldn't be able to sustain for too long. So, with the help of Israeli intelligence, and funding from Saudi Arabia, they began to construct the Wall. It is the Wall of Shame for many reasons. Morally, it is abominable – not only do you take over your neighbour's house, but you also put up a wall to protect your loot. Financially, it is a drain on your increasingly impoverished people. And, most significantly, you are wholly fine with its 'collateral damage': the cost in lives, directly at the wall and indirectly in the narrow sea that separates Africa and Europe.

As a child, I would climb up onto the roof of my house to look east. My stars, the Saharawis who were fighting to liberate us, were in that direction. I tried to see what the grown-ups called the wall. I would climb right up to the top of the concrete steps and risk falling down onto the street. No luck. Just as well my father didn't see me. There was nothing. My favourite brother was behind that invisible wall, that damn wall that made it impossible for me to hug him.

The Wall

The girl would often look east at the stars.
That night, the ochre cloud covered her asteroids.
Don't worry, child, don't cry.
Blow hard,
and you'll see its threat
carried away by the wind.

You'll see its lovely filigree
disintegrate on the horizon.
But although behind the cloud
you may not find Ares, nor Mars,
remember that there are more.
There will always be more.

The wall is really a series of walls that run for about 2,700 km. It isn't a typical wall. It's not like the Berlin Wall. It is a military defensive line inspired by the Bar Lev Line that Israel constructed during the Six-Day War. It took several years to complete the many phases – barbed-wire fencing, radars, bunkers, barricades, anti-personnel minefields, batteries of artillery. The last acquisition, the drones, is also Israel-inspired. These past few months, the drones have claimed the lives of many civilian nomads and innocent livestock.

I was visiting the refugee camps one 27 February – the day when the tribes that make up the Saharawi nation forget their differences and come together under one flag. We demonstrated at the Wall. A few hundred of us carried placards, waving them at the astonished Moroccan soldiers. I noticed a head poking out to observe us through a pair of binoculars. What would he be thinking? Wouldn't he be wondering what he was doing there, so far away from his family and his land, defending the indefensible? Was it just another way of earning a living, for him? As I tried to understand him, there was a commotion – Saharawi soldiers calling out to someone who was trying to rush out beyond the safe zone. On the way back, I saw how the mines could tear metal to pieces. There were remnants of civilian and military vehicles scattered all over. My mind froze at the thought that they would have been driven by human beings.

The Wall

On and on
slithers and hisses
its long, long scar across the land.
Oh, killer
of legends now interred ivory.
From behind, watch hyenas
who came to scatter
clusters of explosives
in the embrace of the hills.
A metal caravan
lies licking and licking
wounds on its side.

The wall did not even help Morocco to win the war. Despite its limited resources, the Saharawi army continued to get around the defensive lines. In 1991, overwhelmed by the military spending, Hassan II sat down with the Saharawi government to sign the Peace Plan, designed by the UN, that included a ceasefire and the organisation of a referendum on self-determination. The United Nations Mission for the Referendum in Western Sahara was created and an envoy of the Secretary-General for the territory was appointed. The refugees began to pack up their belongings into trunks made of asbestos roofing sheets stripped off their mud-brick houses. After nearly a century of Spanish colonisation, 16 years of war and Moroccan occupation, we were finally going to be able to decide our future, to demolish the wall that separated us from land and family.

Then, one by one, the UN envoys resigned. Hassan II had resorted to his favourite tactic: misdirection. His real goal was to end the war that was draining his national budget. It was never the referendum. For Saharawis, our word is sacred.

Nomadic upbringing associates honour and dignity with keeping one's word. Our representatives thought that everyone would abide by the same code. They were very naïve.

For years, we didn't know where our Shark Island was. It was a dark, scary place inhabited by ghosts – we knew that. But not where it was, or what it was really like. After the signing of the Peace Plan, we discovered that it was at the Alcalá de Megunna, or Kelaat M'gouna, when the Moroccan government was forced to free the Saharawi survivors who had spent decades buried deep within its bowels. The way they looked when they emerged gave meaning to the word *zombie*. Today, Alcalá de Megunna, or Kelaat M'gouna, is known for its flower festival. A rose blooms for each soul that was there, though the tourists do not know it.

What the Cat Passed On

Kyung-Sook Shin

Translated from the Korean by Anton Hur

I AM A CAT. The fur that covers my body is almost completely white. You may think I'm a white cat at first, but there's a black streak running from the back of my ears down my spine to my tail. It's why the youngest person in this village, Hari, calls me Spot. Hari is always alone, like me. Because she's one of the few children in the village, yes, but also because she walks with a limp and can't keep up with the others – like me. Hari left this village two years ago with her parents but came back alone. She was fine when she left but limping when she returned. According to what the villagers said while they picked chilli peppers, Hari's parents had settled down in Seoul. Every dawn, they would go to the fish market in Noryangjin in search of the freshest fish to sell at their store. One dawn, as they got up to go to the market auction, Hari happened to wake up early as well, so they had to take her with them in the back seat of their car. On the way back with the cutlassfish, mackerel and pomfret that they'd bought at a good price, a truck sped through a red light and collided with them head on. I couldn't bear listening to the rest of the story, and I left the chilli patch then. But the villagers' voices still carried. I wanted to wash my ears out with the wind, but I still heard them talk about Hari's parents dying on the spot, Hari surviving and being taken to the hospital, and the orphaned one returning to live with her grandmother in the village. Having fled from the north during the Korean War and settled in the village after the armistice, Hari's grandmother never forgot the village where she grew up and the people she had to leave behind – which was why she remained in this village even after Hari's parents left. She'd wanted to spend her remaining days in the village that was closest to where she'd come from, and no one could talk her out of it.

After overhearing her story, I found myself approaching Hari whenever I saw her. If Hari could walk or run away as fast as the other children, I may have overlooked her, too. But she couldn't, and so she was mostly alone. Sitting by herself in the playground after the children had gone home from playing jokgu, or resting under the tree in front of the village community centre, Hari was always alone when I saw her. Sometimes, I would bump into her as she walked slowly across a bridge or through an alley. My habit was to avoid humans, big or little, but once I met Hari, the girl who had returned to the village with a limp, she became the only person I would approach, rubbing against her hurt leg.

The children of this village are always bored. They'd be gathered at one spot and then, seeing something pique their curiosity, dart off as a group to investigate. Hari would be left in the dust, watching the backs of the other children disappear. Then she would slowly get up, after a while, and limp away in the other direction. One day, I followed her as stealthily as I could. She felt like a sympathetic spirit to me, somehow. As a cat, I hate running in the first place. But because I limp like Hari, I can't walk fast, either. Learning her story made me want to approach her, though, and I would go up to her when she was sitting somewhere or follow her as she walked away from the other children. I kept pace with her. It made me feel less afraid, less lonely. When Hari sat by the creek and put her feet in the water, I would find a sunny spot nearby and warm up my fur and yawn. When Hari pulled at the weeds growing by the wall of some house, I found a spot to pee and covered it up with earth. Hari, who had treated me like I was invisible at first, was soon looking around her whenever she was left alone. I knew instinctively that she was looking for me. I would leap out of the grass or come out from behind the tree, meowing and dropping to a roll on the ground, regardless of where we were. That's how I became close to her despite her standoffishness. They say a fox recognises a fox; I don't know what Hari was thinking, but I believe she and I became friends when we recognised we both have this lack, this limp. Hari can't run, and I can follow her only slowly. Between the trees, between the rice paddies, between the houses. I like it when Hari pets the spot on my hip where the black fur pools. When I rub my face against her knees, she says things like, 'The pussy willows are out by the creek. That means spring is coming.' Hari may have her limp that prevents her from running or walking very fast, but she was the first one to know where in the village the flowers were blooming in the spring, when the ice began melting in the creek, and whose rice paddy ripened first in the autumn. It was because she didn't run around like other children that she had plenty of time to gaze at the fields. I always thought Hari was wonderfully aware in that way. But as she looked out in the distance, it was often a sad gaze. She would ask me questions:

'Spot, have you ever gone over to that side?'

The place she pointed to wasn't Daeseong-dong, where we lived, but Kijong-dong.

'My grandmother is sick.'

Her voice was sorrowful.

41

'If I were strong enough, I would've carried Grandmother there...'

I'd never been to Kijong-dong. A long time ago, when I lived in the forests of the Demilitarized Zone with my friends, I could've visited it. But now that I've left that forest, I can barely walk from here to there. The fact that I'm walking so much at all now is thanks to Hari; I'm trying to catch up with her. Because a part of my leg was hurt, it's more of a hop than a walk. And my favourite thing to do is to curl up into a ball and do nothing. But she said this to me:

'You have to walk. If you don't walk just because you're in pain, you'll never walk again.'

I couldn't tell whether Hari was saying this to me or to herself. But I thought she was right. You'll never walk again if you're curled up in a ball all the time.

Anyway, back to my story.

That place Hari asked if I'd ever been to is called Kijong-dong. The name makes it sound like any other ordinary neighbourhood, but it's in North Korea. And Daeseong-dong, where Hari and I live, is in South Korea. When the armistice was declared in 1953, both sides decided to create a civilian village each near the Joint Security Area of Panmunjom, with Daeseong-dong on the South side and Kijong-dong on the North. The two villages are both within the Demilitarized Zone, facing each other at the very edge of the North–South border. I've never been to Kijong-dong and don't know what Daeseong-dong looks like from their side, but Kijong-dong from our side looks like a scattering of grey apartment buildings. Hari's grandmother had fled one of the villages near Kijong-dong during the war and was living on this side now. We would find her gazing north whenever she had a moment to herself, wondering if she'd ever be able to return in her lifetime. When she became sick, Hari would sometimes go up to the roof of the village community centre and stare out at the grey apartments and say to me: 'Hey Spot, you don't think people really live there, right?'

I looked where she was pointing. It did look to me that, unlike Daeseong-dong in the South, no one lived in Kijong-dong. But I've never been there, so who knows. This said, as I'm freer in my movement than humans, I may have to visit that side sometime – just to answer Hari's question, you see. When Hari became interested in the northern side, I also began paying attention to it. There really don't seem to be any people there. Even if there were, they wouldn't be able to visit us: there's a militarised border between the two places. Hari couldn't go there, either. But I'm a cat, and so I'd just have to put my mind to it. I'm a lazy cat, though, and I've only got three whole legs, which disinclines me to make the effort. I'd never given the place a second thought, even though it was a mere 800 metres between the two villages, until the day when Hari asked me in a lonely voice, 'Have you ever been there?'

My eyes are hazel-coloured. I learned that recently. A few days ago, Hari came into the abandoned house in which I was living. It used to belong to her parents, but now no one lives in it. Even when Hari's parents lived in this village, they didn't live with her grandmother. The old lady had no intention of leaving her own house – it affords the clearest view of the North. Her grandmother's tiny home truly does have the best vantage of Kijong-dong. Houses are funny things. Almost everything in the world gets worn down and useless when people handle it too much. But houses are the opposite. When people stop living in them, cobwebs appear immediately, walls become cracked, and cold drafts invade kitchens that seem to decay. This house is no different. Ever since Hari's parents left, it's been falling apart. Hari, when she came back to this village, went to live at her grandmother's house. And this one still stands empty. Hari drew the curtains of the house and stared out the window. Did half an hour pass? She then noticed me purring on the maru porch and came out to sit with me. She looked into my face for a moment and said, 'Your eyes are hazel...' Her voice trailed off, like my cry had the day I realised I had to survive the forest alone. I'd spent a lot of time with Hari by that point, but it was the first time she looked at me with such sadness.

'Spot... Save Grandma.'

But how was I to save her? Hari said, 'If Grandma dies, I'm all alone.' She pointed towards Kijong-dong again and said, 'Grandma wants to be buried there.' She stroked my chin.

Daeseong-dong, where Hari and I live, is not marked on the map. If someone were to put the address into a navigation app in a car, they would be given a *No place found* message. Do you know the other name for this unfindable village? Ironically, it's 'Freedom Village'. And despite its name, there are many restrictions on moving in and out of it, and no one is allowed to own land in it. There are about 50 households and 200 villagers, but it's not a place people can freely visit. Even tourists need a permit to come up here. Villagers, if they ever want to take the bus somewhere, need to report it first-hand and get permission to do so. There are complicated procedures, but it's not impossible. They get deliveries and all that. Once the regiment that manages the place approves you, and you submit a form of ID, you're allowed in. Deliveries are left at the checkpoint where the villagers pick them up. The most interesting scene in this village is when children go to and from school. They're escorted by soldiers with live ammunition. This is the DMZ, after all. It's a common sight to see soldiers guarding the villagers going about the fields with their farming, the latter in the rice paddies and the former standing on the dykes with their rifles. I wonder if there is any other place in the world where you can see that? One time, when the tomatoes were ripening and I was in the fields hoping for one, the tomato farmer pulled up with some soldiers in a truck and began picking them. He tossed some to the soldiers and they wiped them on their clothes and gobbled them up. It's not just the tomatoes they share, for sure.

Everyone who lives here must be present to be counted in the evening, and when they come back from trips outside the village they must report in. If there's anyone missing at the nightly headcounts, an emergency is declared. It's just like how soldiers get counted before lights off at the barracks. We do live a mere 800 metres from North Korea. Daeseong-dong may be on South Korean land, but it's managed by the United Nations, and the villagers don't pay taxes to the Korean government. Healthy Korean men must serve in the military when they're of age, but not the men of Daeseong-dong. Anyone born in Daeseong-dong must decide by the age of thirty-one whether they will live in the village or move out. If they leave, all the privileges and obligations of the village cease for them, and they become an ordinary South Korean citizen.

Hari will make that choice when she turns 31 as well, won't she? The prospect frightens me. Will I live to see the day she turns 31? I guess it's pointless for me to think of such things. I'm just a cat after all... A cat's life is much shorter than any human's.

Freedom Village, which I am allowed to wander about at will, is bound by all sorts of rules and limitations. Control is key, which means development is regulated, too. The people who live here have no right to buy and sell things like houses or fields. Even if their ageing roofs start leaking, they can't just fix them on their own. They need to get permission. Rains might take out entire roads, but they can't just repave them. Every little discrepancy in the way roads and fields are recorded must be accounted for and corrected. Every little change needs to be granted permission. Naturally, this cuts off the village from the outside world. It's like time stopped here. There are, as I said earlier, around 200 villagers. They live in full view of North Korea. A village called Freedom, but there are no freedoms. I'm sure Kijong-dong is no different. Perhaps they have even fewer freedoms than we do. But Hari's grandmother wants to be buried there. I understand how she feels. It's because she never said a proper goodbye when she left, thinking she would be on the southern side for a brief spell until the war ended, not imagining she would never set foot in her birthplace again.

I didn't always live in Daeseong-dong. I was born in the forests of the DMZ. I haven't been back since I left, but I do think of the place once in a while. What? My story makes you want to visit? I knew you would. This pandemic has made me realise how much humans love to travel. Once the borders were closed and no one could go anywhere overseas, all sorts of strange little travel options popped up, I heard. Like taking an aeroplane to the skies above a foreign city and looking down at it before flying back home. What kind of travel is that? But people who took it loved it. Hearing those stories about people looking down at the cities they wanted to visit and eating their meals and taking a nap in the aeroplanes made me think how it would be impossible to take away people's desire for movement. Travel is something lazy animals like cats will never understand. Officially, outsiders can't visit here without the permission of UN Command, but if you really wanted to come, there's a way. You might find the peacefulness of the path surprising, though. It's very different to what you might expect of these parts. But humans are astonishingly good at adapting to their environments. Who would live in a place with so many rules? Humans! Every day, and in peace and quiet at that.

It's thanks to Hari's family that I began to like humans. Come to think of it, it was Hari's mother who first put out cat food for me. When she lived in this house, I slept in the warehouse of the community centre. Hari's mother always kept fresh water and dry cat food for me by the garden wall of this house. That's not all: from time to time, she would get permission to leave the village to go to the market in Paju and buy cat food. It's the closest place you can go from this village by bus. She'd go all the way there and back, filling up my bowl with food. I think I moved in here after they left because I missed Hari's mother. Hari didn't come here after she lost her parents, and neither did her grandmother. Well, they couldn't, even if they wanted to. The memories would probably have been too painful for them. The things that had happened to Hari were too much for a little one to fathom. Like my children. They only have their breakfasts with me. Aside from my time with Hari, I gather things to eat all day and put them beneath the maru porch, waiting for the morning. My babies are only five months old but they have to find their own food already, because of their mother's leg being what it is. Most people in this village ignore my children. We're just cats to them. Although sometimes they see that I have a limp and go inside to get me a treat. Naturally, I've developed a routine in gathering food. On Tuesdays and Wednesdays, I go into the woods near the village. There's a beekeeper who spends Tuesdays and Wednesdays in a tent there. Remember when I said that soldiers stand by guarding the farmers when tomatoes are being harvested? This is a common sight. Not strange at all, here. The beekeeper and soldiers bring me and my children into the tent and give us food – things like hardtacks and tuna cans. It's tastier than dry cat food, and my children go wild eating it up. That takes care of Tuesdays and Wednesdays; on Thursdays, we have to go deeper north into the woods. There's a Jindo dog there named Yongja. Every Wednesday night, a man comes to a shipping container in the woods, and until he comes back, Yongja guards the container. Yongja's house nearby is very wide. There are five bowls of food, plenty of water, a roof that shelters the dog from rain and snow, and a separate room for Yongja to sleep in. On Thursdays, the man fills up the five food bowls and the water. I don't know what he does in these woods. He stays in the shipping container by the doghouse and sometimes plants trees and other times moves rocks from here to there. He also has a vegetable patch where he grows chillies, cucumbers, and tomatoes. The strange thing is that, while the beekeeper is guarded by the police, this man is left alone. Maybe he is not a villager, but a secret agent with a mission. In any case, he leaves behind enough food and water for a week. Yongja, as if trained to do so, eats only one bowl of food a day. I thought this was something only cats were clever enough to do, but here's a dog doing it. One day, I was watching Yongja being fed when the man noticed me and put out some food for me, too. A generous amount, I should say – it was for me, but was enough for all my children as well. To my children, with whom I only have breakfast, I always say: 'Don't fill up your bellies just because you see lots of food in front of you. You have to stop after you've had your fill – not to leave some for the next day, but to train yourself to survive in this village having eaten as little as possible. Just in case.'

Hari, who rarely visited her parents' old house before the summer vacation, now comes from time to time to sit in the empty rooms. She seems sad, and the only thing I can do for her is to sit by her. She occasionally strokes my neck. Aside from her visits, this house is mostly empty.

Does Hari know? Does she know that when I was about as old as my children, my leg was injured? Back then, I didn't live in the village, but in the DMZ forest with my friends. We were all orphans. I don't know how we found each other, but we were definitely together. No similarities, everyone born in different places from different parents, but our days lively and free. If the rock in the forest hadn't fallen, we might still be living there. That day, we'd left for a trip to the mountains, up a path we'd never gone on before. It was right after the rains had come and the paths were slippery. There were trees collapsed all over the forest, and great chunks of yellow earth jutting out menacingly here and there. We walked, our senses sharp, and upon the cry of a bird overhead, started to run. It was like a rain cloud had come over us when everything went dark. Then, a large rock crashed down. My friends managed to get away, but I was almost crushed underneath. I managed to swerve just in time, but it hit my side. I don't remember how I survived. When I came to, it was night and there was darkness everywhere. Stars looked down on me. I began limping from then on. I lost all feeling in that leg and couldn't put my paw down. It curled into me, toes and all. I don't know what happened to my friends or what they're doing now. No matter how long I wandered that forest, I couldn't find them. I wonder if they're still together? Not being able to walk, I couldn't look for them any further, and by the time my leg had healed somewhat, I realised that I was left all alone in that forest. The thought made my shoulders sag, but I told myself I needed to keep my wits about me. I had to survive on one less leg now. I managed to leave the forest and enter the village. I could've gone to Kijong-dong instead of Daeseong-dong, but I didn't really choose. I limped to where my feet were taking me, and I found myself in Daeseong-dong.

I want to tell Hari my story.

The first thing I did upon leaving the forest where I had frolicked to my heart's content was to forget how to run. This wasn't easy. I'd find myself breaking into a sprint like I used to before my injury and stopping in my tracks from the pain. How much I want to tell Hari of all the things I learned in exchange for forgetting how to run! Of the acorns, the snails, and the flower seeds I'd seen when I slowed down. That even if she loses her grandmother, there are miraculous days ahead of her. I may have lost my ability to climb trees, but when I sit under trees or on soft moss that covers rocks, tree leaves fall and cover my paws. I want to tell Hari that she'll be able to go to the family her grandmother had left behind, someday, over there in Kijong-dong. I want to tell her that though I'd forgotten how to run, I couldn't forget the friends I made in the forest – which is why we need to get along with our friends and loved ones, and why, when it comes to relationships that inevitably must end, we need to know how to say goodbye. Hari doesn't know this, but some nights, when the moon is up, I climb up to the roof of this empty house and think about the friends I never got to say goodbye to. Are they all right? Are they staring at the moon? Are they thinking of me, too? When I first came down to this village from the forests of the DMZ, I would hide in mailboxes or warehouses. And as I crouched there staring out at the endless rain, or the thick snow that piled higher and higher, I would think of my friends. If I'd parted with them well, I would've smiled whenever I thought of them. But instead, thinking of my friends makes me lonely. Because we never said goodbye properly. Cats or humans, we all need to say goodbye properly, or our lives become too lonely. When the rock fell in the forest and my leg was pinned down beneath it, I stared at my spooked friends who had leaped away to safety. How could I have said goodbye to them properly then, I think. That was the moment I became truly alone.

Life in this village isn't easy. My wish is to live quietly and die quietly. But, one day, I met the one who followed the beekeeper into the forest, and we spent some time together. Even if he ended up leaving me as well. And under the maru of this empty house, I gave birth to our three children. I didn't breastfeed my children for long. I couldn't give much milk, and my children had to go out into the woods and get their own food. They're all small now, perhaps because of this. The only survival skill I could teach them was to not eat all the food they see before them and to think of tomorrow. Useless advice, really. Ever since Hari's mother left this village, we've never had enough to eat, so what's the use of telling my children not to eat something? Aside from our breakfast, I have no idea what my children eat or where they eat it, but they're still growing well. None of them have limps, and the three of them stick together and seem to enjoy running and frolicking in the woods. Wherever they go, they come running when I call them in the morning at dawn. Running through the pine trees and maple trees and through the mossy undergrowth. They nip at my empty breasts as we tumble together, which is our morning hello. No matter how deep the night, no matter how stormy, the morning always comes. The morning where I can see my children again. I wait for every morning. The food I've gathered is always inadequate, but I dole it out among them and clean them and paw them and nuzzle their ears and they run away and I chase them. And we go up on the garden wall of this empty house and take a nap under the sun. And then we scatter.

Today, I've come to Hari's grandmother's house, because Hari refuses to come outside. For the past five days, Hari's grandmother has only been drinking water, refusing all food and even to wash her face. Hari sits by her, exhausted, occasionally placing the back of her hand on her grandmother's forehead. The villagers come with dotorimuk or taro and perilla soup and bid her to eat while it's hot, but Hari's grandmother can't eat any of it. Her breathing is irregular. The people tell her she needs to go to the hospital. But the grandmother shakes her head and only stares at Hari, thinking, perhaps, of what is to become of her granddaughter when she's left behind on her own. One night, very late, Hari gets her grandmother to sit up. She leans over and whispers in her grandmother's ear.

'Grandmother, I'll take you there.'

I stare at Hari from outside her door. She puts her thin grandmother on her back. My heart is in my mouth as I watch her unsteadily make her way towards me. Surely she will topple over before she reaches the threshold. Even if she manages to get herself down to the maru and out the gate, she couldn't possibly make her way out of the village. The soldiers would discover them and escort them back home. But I want Hari to go as far as she can go, and so I am following her, urging her on. I have a thought: that Hari carrying her grandmother all the way to Kijong-dong, to the land that her grandmother so longed to see for all these years, may be impossible, but that Hari trying as hard as she can to make it happen is her way of saying goodbye. Hari, who told me my eyes were hazel, is very slowly coming out of the room with her grandmother on her back. Powerless as I am, I quickly fall in line behind them. I want to guard Hari like the soldiers guard the tomato farmers. I don't know what's going to happen to Hari now, but I want to pass on something to her, this girl who told me my eyes were hazel. That she is saying goodbye to her grandmother and saying it well. That just as there are mornings that a mere cat like me looks forward to, such mornings will find their way to her. That, someday, she too will be able to go to that village beyond Kijong-dong.

But for now, the night is dark and endless.

This Side of the Wall

Juan Pablo Villalobos

Translated from the Spanish by Rosalind Harvey

THE FIRST WALL WAS the one around my parents' house, in a village in Mexico in the 1980s. I was ten years old when we were kicked out of our rented home and my father decided to build, very hurriedly, a house in a new development up on the hill. Since we were going to be the only people on the block – there was quite literally nothing at all in the surrounding area – Dad thought it necessary to erect a perimeter wall. Initially, more than protecting us from external threats, this wall served to mark the limits of the garden around the house, preventing the owners of the adjacent plots, when they did eventually build their houses, from encroaching onto ours. The truth was, our neighbours-to-be were two sisters and a brother of my father's, which made the construction of the wall an even more pressing matter, because it was possible any hypothetical conflict might acquire epic proportions. But let's not get ahead of ourselves.

The new house was big, but it wasn't luxurious. It was big for a big family: Dad, my mum, my four siblings, our mad dog, a fluctuating number of cats, two pairs of lovebirds, the multiple exotic animals my younger brother was forever adopting (hawks, coyotes, salamanders, rabbits, iguanas, guinea pigs), and me. What I mean is that it wasn't a mansion, was in fact far from being such a thing. For instance: the first time there was a serious downpour, every single one of the rooms sprung a leak, because Dad's money had run out and he'd put off weatherproofing the building until later.

'It's not the rainy season,' Dad kept saying, defending himself, despite the buckets all around us gradually filling up with rain and Mum's tears.

Dad was a GP – he's retired now – and would spend all day, every day working in his office, except for Sunday afternoons. Mum's job was raising us and working on the assembly line of domestic life: cooking, cleaning, laundry, shopping. We all studied at a religious school, our beach holidays were as frequent as visits from the bishop (once every three or four years, so you get an idea), and we bought our clothes in the local shop; the only imported products we had were brought over by Dad's sister, who had emigrated to the other side of the border wall. But we did have a video cassette player, an encyclopaedia, a subscription to *Reader's Digest,* cable TV, and membership of a sports club, where we took swimming and tennis lessons. I mention all this because it's important always to make clear from where one is writing, from which place: from within or from without the wall. And because walls are not static: they move, they have a life of their own.

Beyond the wall of the new house were only uncultivated plots where the weeds grew rampant; Dad's siblings didn't bother to look after their bits of land. Despite its height, the wall did not protect us from all the pests that crept into the garden – rats, vipers, cockroaches, geckos – which were astonished to discover the wonderful life my younger brother gave all his exotic pets. The weeds in the empty plots flourished at the same rate as Mum and Dad's paranoia: they envisioned thieves hiding in the bushes, scaling a wall and breaking into our house. And so Dad asked a builder to install a highly sophisticated security system on top of the wall: a crown of jagged pieces of broken glass from bottles – essentially, the same idea as concertinas, the coiled barbed wire which the Spanish government, to give just one example, uses to protect the border of Melilla with Morocco.

One of the owners of the neighbouring plots of land was Dad's sister, the one who lived on the other side of the border wall, my aunt from the other side. She was planning to build a house there in a little while, when her husband – also Mexican-American, a veteran of the Korean War – retired. She used to come and visit in the summer, her suitcases filled with goods the family had requested in those years before the North American Free Trade Agreement. Clothes, toys, perfume, sports equipment, small household appliances. She would stay in my grandparents' house, and the day she arrived you had to be really patient until she agreed to open her bags and share out all her purchases. It was obvious she enjoyed making us beg, delaying the moment, making us feel her power; she was the wall that separated our Third World status from the First World.

'Auntie, when are you going to open your suitcases?' we would say.

'Oh,' she would reply in English (she loved to do this), 'so you don't actually want to see me? You only love me because I bring you things?'

My geopolitical consciousness, and that of my siblings and cousins, was formed in this period, by way of these small moments of emotional blackmail: we lived on this side of the wall, the wrong side, and we had to be patient, caring, respectful, stoical, if we wanted to be rewarded by my aunt, who acted like a representative of the World Bank and the International Monetary Fund.

Accompanying my father's sister were her four children, two girls and two boys – my cousins from the other side. My siblings, my cousins and I tried to communicate with them, but we struggled due to the language barrier; they spoke very little Spanish (it seemed as if they were ashamed of being half Mexican) – and the English we'd learned at school was pretty poor. And as if that wasn't enough, there were insurmountable cultural differences, too: we liked heavy metal music, which they claimed was the devil's work. (In honour of the truth, I should open this parenthesis, because the truth is always complicated, especially in literature, and it's my duty to note here that one of those cousins is now an expert in Mayan culture and knows more about pre-Hispanic peoples than all of us, the Mexican cousins. Something of his reticence persists, however, because he still lives on the other side, has a very good post at a Californian university, and comes to visit Mexico only for research or to accompany his students.)

As soon as my aunt from the other side handed over her purchases, our social status would change: we'd move a little bit further up the scale. The following day, that toy or bit of sports kit would make us momentarily equal to the people we knew who went shopping in San Antonio or Laredo, San Diego or Tucson. The problem was that my aunt from the other side would only come over to this side once every two years, give or take, which restricted our social mobility.

After we had opened the packages with the shopping in and were just settling into a good mood, the adults would order us to take our cousins from the other side for a walk in grandfather's orchard. This was ten hectares of land, filled with fruit trees and with a perimeter wall more beautiful than any I've seen in my life: a hedgerow made of fig trees. On the other side was the train line and the Nestlé factory, which in the 1950s had kickstarted the process of industrialisation of this rural village. On that side lay the future, modernity: powdered milk, sugary cereals, artificially flavoured dairy products; on this side, protected by the row of figs, the anticipatory nostalgia of that garden, the symbol of the childhood we were losing (Nestlé had in fact purchased part of this land from my grandfather, who had used the money to acquire the land up on the hill, which he had divided up and shared out amongst his children – but that's another story).

As we walked around amongst the apple trees, the peach trees, the grenadine trees and the lemon trees, my siblings, my cousins from this side and I grilled our cousins from the other side about what the other side was like: we wanted to know what they had that we didn't. We wanted them to tell us about the malls and the shops, about the theme parks and the sports stadiums, but they insisted that the difference lay in how people behaved. According to them, it was cleaner over there. People respected laws and justice was always served. There, if you worked hard, you could buy yourself anything you wanted, get a new car every year, go on holiday to visit your family in the Third World. Not here. Here there were only grubby streets, hunger, devaluation, inflation, bitterness, resentment, satanic rituals.

Then we reached the edge of grandfather's orchard and started eating figs.

'Did Grandfather say you could do that?' our cousins from the other side would ask, staring as we assaulted the fig trees.

We didn't answer, partly because we couldn't really understand them, and partly because our mothers had taught us not to speak with our mouths full. I remember seeing how tempted the smallest of the cousins looked, although his siblings held him back, because the figs hadn't even been washed.

We returned to our grandparents' house, where my cousins from the other side spoke in English to my aunt from the other side and we were punished for having swiped fruit from the fig trees. Dad took our gifts away, declassing us immediately. And then we all got a stomach ache.

Almost twenty years later, in 1998, when I was 25, I went to visit a girlfriend who had gone to study in Tijuana and finally got to see the wall of walls, the border of Mexico with the United States. We weren't going to cross over to the other side – I didn't have a visa or a passport at the time – but one afternoon while we were taking a walk on the beach, we stood for a while looking out at the posts which ran down from the sand towards the water until they disappeared on the horizon, separating the two countries by land and sea. It was such a ridiculous image it made you want to laugh and cry at the same time. No wall, not even an underwater one, had managed to stop stories from flowing from one side to the other of the border.

The history of my dad's family with the other side wasn't just limited to his sister. Grandfather emigrated to the other side of the border wall when he was young and still unmarried – in the 1920s – and his two younger brothers did, too; but Grandfather was the only one who came back, because he didn't like what he saw and experienced in California. His two brothers stayed, got married, had children and grandchildren. As a matter of fact, the youngest took part in the Second World War, and ended up being murdered after some shady business in Sacramento in the 1970s – there's a novel there, one that I'm not going to write – or not now, anyway.

My grandfather, though, returned to Mexico and married my grandmother, and they had nine children – six girls and three boys – including my father. If Grandfather had found the other side to his liking, if he had glimpsed a future of progress and happiness; if, when weighing up whether to stay on the other side or return to this side, his calculations had nudged him, as they do most people, towards staying there, then none of us – my father, my aunts and uncles, my siblings, my cousins, and I – would ever have existed, and I would not be here, writing these memories of the other side. We are the children and grandchildren of Grandfather's failed migration.

Back then – in 1998, I mean, not in 1920 – I was going through an existential crisis and thought that the only way to escape it was by changing my life. I had emigrated from my village to the city to go to university, and now I had a very good job which made me very unhappy. That trip to Tijuana turned out to be a rite of passage, and this perhaps is why I had stared so obsessively at those fence posts sunk into the sea, as if I could swim out and around them and start from scratch somewhere else, that is, abandon my job, go back to university to study literature, and begin to write.

And almost 20 years later – in this story everything happens 18 or 19 years later, but odd numbers don't sound as good – it turned out that I was making a living from writing. It was 2017 and the President of the United States had promised to build more wall, more and more, all along the border, to leave us hopelessly confined to this side here. The plan for the wall was merely the culmination of what was happening on this side, because Mum and Dad's paranoia had turned out to be true (sometimes the paranoid have a point) – the monopoly on violence here was now held by organised crime and drugs cartels, and the crisis of public safety meant that everyone wanted a perimeter wall, an electrified fence, their own personal rolls of barbed wire.

I couldn't stop thinking about one of the little girls I had interviewed a year earlier (in 2016; apologies for jumping around in time so much) for a book I was writing about young refugees. The girl was twelve years old, and her story was very similar to that of the ten other girls and boys I was able to speak to that summer. Stories of children who crossed rivers and deserts – nature's walls – to flee from poverty, family breakdown, male violence, and gangs. A combination that makes life impossible, and which pushes thousands of young people to try to escape the fatal outcome the future seems to hold in store for them.

The girl had put on a smart yellow dress because she thought the interview was going to be on TV. She seemed to be used to telling her story; she told it quickly, her voice shaking, her breath ragged, and with a tone of voice far too childlike for her age – perhaps a way of protecting herself from reality, from a premature loss of innocence. She mixed in a few English words here and there, a mark of the transformation she had been going through ever since she arrived in the United States for a new life. She been born in Guatemala and had emigrated at the age of ten, along with her brother, who was sixteen and being threatened by gangs. They made the journey alone, having slipped out of their aunt's house with the idea of going to find their mum, who had been living in Los Angeles since 2007. The little girl hadn't seen her mum since she was three years old. You could say that she didn't know her. She could not, in fact, remember her.

They crossed Mexico without using one of the people smugglers known as coyotes, instead getting help from locals, asking how to reach Tijuana. They gave themselves up at the San Ysidro checkpoint. Two years later they had acquired the papers to prove that their lives were in danger if they ever returned to Guatemala. Now, they lived with their mother. They were in school. They were happy.

'A boy in school told me that now that Donald Trump's going to win, we're all going to be deported, and our parents, too,' the little girl told me that June afternoon of the previous year. 'And one of my teachers said that she hopes Donald Trump does win so we all get deported. She said we don't have any right to be here.'

'Your teacher told you that?' asked one of the lawyers from the NGO who had helped me set up the interview.

'That's illegal,' said the other lawyer.

'Don't worry,' I broke in, 'Donald Trump isn't going to win.'

'No, of course not,' the two lawyers assured her.

'I know,' said the little girl.

And then it turned out that we were all wrong, and we had to grapple with the consequences. Various forms of media, literary magazines, newspapers, asked me to write about the wall but I always said no, that I needed time, that I needed perspective to write, a bit of distance, maybe not twenty years, but certainly ten, let's say. One particularly sad morning, however, after reading the news on my phone and feeling dreadfully sad, and very angry, so furious I wanted to punch a wall, I sat down to write, and this is what came out:

Let's build the wall. But we'll build it, those of us on this side, and we'll install first aid stations, shelters with doctors, drinking water, food, beds to rest and regain one's strength, English classes. And most importantly: we'll put lots of doors along the length of the wall, thousands of them, doors that only have a handle on this side.

Let's build the wall. But first we'll request a loan to do so from the United States government or the World Bank. Better yet: from the International Monetary Fund. We'll send out a tender for the architectural design, another for the construction and another for the management of the wall once it's finished. We'll only invite tenders, naturally, from friends. And the tenders that win will be those put forward by the very best friends among all the friends. The ones working on the architectural design will delay for a long time, a really long time: years; they're mediocre architects, but they're our best friends. The construction will start years after it was meant to. And then there'll be problems with the construction permits. And more problems with the suppliers of materials. And the workers will go on strike. The first part that's built will start showing cracks and damp spots after just two months, which will mean temporarily suspending construction. Years will pass like this and, with a little bit of luck, the presidents of the United States will also pass, until one comes to power who's not interested in building a wall. Better yet: until one comes to power who orders the construction of the wall to be stopped. We won't return the money of the loan, obviously.

Let's build the wall. A green wall, an eco-friendly one, a hedge. A hedge, to be precise, of marijuana plants. Let's legalise marijuana first, of course, to be used in the construction of walls. Let's see then how flows of migration changes: people from the north coming down in droves to the south, to smoke our wall. Contrary to what you might expect, we will not stop them. On the contrary. We will all meet at the border, and a new era of friendship and fraternity between the two sides will dawn.

Let's build the wall. But let's build it as a tourist attraction, as a theme park. We'll call it the 'The Wall of Shame,' or something along those lines. We'll open museums of racism, imperialism, discrimination. And observation points to see from far away how things are on each side of the wall. It will attract tourists from Japan, China, Germany, Scandinavia, the whole world. Our wall will be a wonderful business and will create thousands of jobs. Jobs that will be filled, of course, by the refugees who cannot cross the wall.

Let's build the wall. An invisible wall, like the

emperor's invisible clothes. A wall only intelligent people can see. We'll build it ourselves, the people on this side, with invisible bricks and invisible mortar, too. Freed from material restrictions, we will make it incredibly tall: 1000 metres tall. And incredibly thick: two kilometres thick. On the day we inaugurate it, we will say to the President of the United States: 'Here is your wall – it's very tall, and very wide, but only intelligent people can see it.' I'm sure that the President of the United States will be most satisfied with it.

I sent the text to my father. Let's hope your aunt doesn't read it, was his reply.

The Fence

Krisztina Tóth

Translated from the Hungarian by Peter Sherwood

I SCRAMBLED DOWNSTAIRS IN my pyjamas. My parents were already up. The scene was weird and scary at the same time. We stood blinking under the garage's striplight, staring at its head. Because that was all you could see, the head that it had forced through the cat-flap while chasing the cat. And though it managed to push the flap in, when it tried to pull its head out, it had got hopelessly stuck: neither in nor out. The fur around its ears was covered in blood. My mother grabbed hold of the dog and started pushing it from behind. No luck. Then she tried to coax it to pull its ears back and squeeze through, but it was at an impossible angle. All the squealing had by now woken up the neighbours, who were out on the upstairs balconies with their lights switched on.

'Hey, mind the garage door! Leave it the fuck alone! Just cut it off!'

'You mean cut its head off?' My father, incredulous, turned in the direction of the voice. The neighbour was shivering in his dressing gown and just wanted the noise to stop. My mother burst into tears and kept kicking and pushing the door and then, for some reason, wrapped a blanket round the dog, thinking it might be cold.

'You think she might be thirsty?' she asked.

My father was beside himself at the dog: 'Fucking stupid bitch!' In the end, the next-door neighbour, a joiner by day, rustled up a chainsaw, and they set to work. My mother held the tightly wrapped body from behind, while I squatted down next to it inside the doorway. I tried to soothe the creature, but there was no point: by then she was past hearing anything, whimpering away with her eyes rolled back in her head, her drool flowing down onto the concrete. The sun was up by the time we finished.

'I'm going to murder that fucking cat,' my father commented on the night's events as he put the chainsaw back by the boiler.

Still, in the morning that fucking cat turned up at the usual time for its raw liver, the only thing it had deigned to eat for some time now. It surveyed disdainfully the debris of the night's mayhem – the blanket and what remained of the garage door by the wall – then padded over to my mother's feet to await the clink of its dish on the floor.

The dog, on the other hand, wouldn't eat. For two whole days it refused to come out from under the table and wouldn't allow itself to be touched. It trembled all the time, its nose was dry, and its eyes had an oily glow. Only its empty plastic bowl indicated that it was, nonetheless, prepared to drink some water. This was when, in my mother's opinion, the dog stopped growing – 'from the shock,' she'd said. Though to be honest, I had my suspicions about the dog even before this happened. A German shepherd from prize-winning parents, fifth of the litter – but no proof of pedigree.

When we first brought her home, this whelp of prize-winning parents pissed all over my coat, only to spend the next two months rapidly and seriously getting stronger and growing – though, it should be said, only horizontally. Its legs didn't get any longer, and the whole dog began to resemble a dachshund, one that had been whimsically crowned with the head of a German Shepherd; its velvety antenna-ears were entirely out of proportion to the breed. The drunks hanging around the off-licence next door soon grew fond of the pup behind the railings with its high-pitched squeal, and kept shouting: 'Shut the fuck up, bat-ears!'

By the age of one, it was as tall as it would ever be: mid-calf height. Its ancestry – since the owner of its parents with their alleged distinguished bloodline never again made an appearance at the market – remained shrouded in obscurity: dachshunds, German shepherds, retrievers, and fox-terriers chased after one another, and the hares, in their dreams, endlessly whirl on the obscure terrain of genetics.

The dog was forever hanging around my father, getting under his feet when he came rolling up with the wobbly wheelbarrow from the back garden or burning piles of leaf mould. Even though she was afraid of the smoke and kept shaking her head and snorting and spluttering, there she would be again the next time he made the trip, sniffing around my father's rubber boots. In high summer, they would relax side by side, but the dog was on the alert even when it was napping, and if it heard some suspicious sound would run grunting and wheezing over to the gate and then, alarm over, return to hunker down in the shadow of its master's belly.

My father's belly was enormous, criss-crossed by deep scars the colour of mother-of-pearl that were only slightly obscured by the blond hairs across his stomach and chest. One of the scars, the main trail, wound its way as far as his collarbone. It was traversed by three crossroads, one at the chest, another just above the navel, and a third lower down. On his back, too, there were two craters, sewn up with enormous stitches. My father had been covered with these mysterious trails since before I was born; they led somewhere deep inside him, into that dark and silent forest of which he never spoke. For our part, we never asked where these trails came from and where they led, simply acknowledging their existence: the story of the accident. How often we had heard the story of the car skidding on the icy road, spinning round and crashing into another as it spilled out all its passengers.

He told this story any number of times, always with the same, tried and tested turns of phrase, whenever someone asked about those horrendous scars – and people very often did. He'd played water polo in his younger days and even though he'd try to grab his towel and cover up the scars, his teammates would always rib him mercilessly in the showers: 'Not the Grim Reaper after you, was it?' He would laugh along with them and say: 'Yeah, it was, but he couldn't swim fast enough!' And he would have to tell the story of that icy road yet again, for the hundredth time.

In fact, these days only his broad shoulders would remind anyone of his water polo playing days, his belly having since rounded out and expanded exponentially. For my father loved his food, guzzling down – indiscriminately and to excess – everything put in front of him, as if trying to make up for all the times he had been left hungry as a child. In this respect he was very much like the dog, which also made sure that the chunks of food it was fed disappeared in a flash, without even being chewed, and if you tried to slow things down by serving the food a little at a time, its pointed nose would sniff out and hoover up the surrounding terrain in seconds.

In the past it had managed to swallow burst balloons, bits of tennis balls, plastic watchstraps, and even carrier bags. As the bags proved impossible to evacuate in the normal way, the vet had to scrape them out of the creature's blocked intestines after it had been retching for days on end.

No wonder it watched my father with great empathy, head cocked to one side, as he demolished his third helping of cabbage and pig knuckle, sweating profusely in the summer heat, and bent over the terrace handrail. 'I'll be fine,' he said, more to the dog than to my mother, as both awaited developments. Then, somehow, he dragged himself indoors and went to lie down, but failed to surface even once the midday heat had passed. Or even by evening. On the contrary, he became increasingly shivery, had to wrap himself in several blankets, and moaned pitifully. My mother kept changing the icepacks as she reeled off, at great length and with much sighing, all the things my father ought not to have eaten to avoid the consequences that, as he could surely see, had now befallen him, and might indeed have befallen him much earlier, after the rabbit, the stuffed cabbage, and the cheap booze that had been served up at Dezső's. Meanwhile, she brought him bowls of water with increasing frequency, because by around midnight the compresses would be bone dry in a matter of minutes. In the middle of the night, he suddenly sat up, stopped moaning, and declared he wanted to make his will, at which point my mother decided to call for an ambulance.

The gall bladder operation was successful. My father felt better; we just had to wait for the results of the scan. They found shadows on his liver, which had to be checked out. They might be cysts; we'd soon know for sure. A week later the doctor called my mother in. He asked her about that car crash long ago: what exactly had happened? It would be helpful if she could dig out the paperwork because the adhesions suggested that further intervention would be needed. My mother was alarmed by the word 'intervention', her nerves being further put on edge by the grim-faced doctor who looked her in the eye all the time, as if trying to catch her out. The shadows on the liver, the doctor remarked on his way out, appeared to be pieces of shrapnel, at which my mother stared at him blankly, either because she couldn't place the word 'shrapnel' out of context, or because she'd just realised she forgot to hand over the brown envelope she'd been clutching and out in the corridor no longer dared to. So, it would be good to get hold of the discharge note issued after the accident, because in my father's stomach they'd found some growths which were – and here he had looked at my mother again – distinctly odd and which we might be clearer about if we knew more about the circumstances.

He left, but my mother stayed sitting in the corridor for a while and only then went back into the ward.

'Dr. Gyarmathy,' my father managed to murmur, 'but he may no longer be alive.'

But Dr. Gyarmathy was very much alive and met my mother wearing a jacket and white shirt. He was well into his nineties but ramrod straight. Only later, after half an hour's conversation, did he start playing the role of the senile old man with memory loss – in my mother's view, none too convincingly.

He hadn't been easy to find. He had retired to a remote village, far from the border; it had taken two weeks to track him down. Who knows how my mother managed to persuade him to see her. Perhaps he wanted to see, before he died, what had happened to that loose end he had failed to tie up, the life that in the 1956 Revolution he had, in his despair, unwittingly turned upside down.

'I can't remember,' he said. 'I'm really sorry, my good lady, but I just can't remember.' Yet he remembered that night all too clearly: for years it had dominated his dreams, and whenever he heard steps on the pavement outside at night, or felt a shudder when on a night call, he would think: *That's it, the story continues*, because he knew that stories never end, they are only broken off and lie low, like latent diseases, only to resurface and spread, resulting in stabs of pain elsewhere, only for that pain to be passed down from generation to generation.

And although he might sometimes be able to put a name to the illness and treat the resurgent pain, he didn't know what to do about those stories that circulated endlessly, as in the case of this woman: what on earth could he do about her? About the fragments of shrapnel lodged in the man's liver, the decades of silence, the trauma that lingered, ingrained?

There'd been fourteen of them, nine adults and five children. My father was thirteen at the time, the other kids were a year or two older. But this was not obvious, because despite his size he was the most capable of them all, the one who had always to look after his six younger siblings, and gradually he grew and filled those shoes. He didn't stand out from the big lads, and perhaps they didn't even know he was younger. He joined the others because he'd heard that the West was the Promised Land. The borders were open, you could just leave. Right through the chaotic days of the Revolution, the family had stayed with relatives in a village near the border. At least there you could get food even when the bigger cities were running short. His mother, my grandma, didn't really understand what was going on. Even before, she'd known precious little about politics: she simply brought one child after another into the world and all the chaos and brawling in the family was driving her out of her mind. She did nothing but cook noodles in a big pot and yell at the kids.

My father had had enough of looking after his brothers and sisters, enough of the noodles, of the rags they were dressed in. He decided to escape with the others and set off for the border.

The group woke the local doctor at daybreak. They were village folk, a noisy lot, and rattled the windows. They said they'd been woken around two in the morning by the sound of gunfire, but none of them dared go outside. They'd waited indoors in silence, whispering, guessing, praying, and then, in the grey light of dawn, the men got dressed and did go out into the fields after all. Fourteen people were lying on the ground, all young folk from the neighbourhood. None of them was breathing any longer, but there was a trail of blood across the frozen ground suggesting that one had been about to set off, perhaps back home, across the fields. Silence enveloped them. Some lay face down, others on their backs, their clothes covered in the hoarfrost of the early dawn. There were no tears or wailing from the men or, oddly enough, from the few women who ventured out after them. They spoke in short, quiet sentences. The truck came and they piled on the dead. And when all the bodies were on the truck, you could see that one of the bodies stirred.

It was my father.

The men banged on the doctor's window: Do something! The very old man that stood across from my mother today was then a young doctor at the beginning of his career. He looked out: what on earth could they be wanting at this hour?

A wave of anger and despair swept over the men and seemed to be channelled towards the doctor, as if it was all his fault: 'that rabble', they kept saying, as they shot him such murderous glances that he almost began to be afraid of the men in heavy boots pushing and shoving around him. It was the Russians, they shouted, they've closed the border.

My father still had a pulse. They carried him over to the summer kitchen; blood was oozing from his mouth and trailed along the stone flags at the entrance and into the inner courtyard. Lights went on in the nearby cottages, but the group ignored them and waited in silence in front of the summer kitchen to see what would happen next. The doctor called out to one of the men and together they carried the body into the house. 'They 'ave to op'rate,' one of the women reported back.

The operation was carried out on the dining room table.

My father had been struck by four bullets: two had passed straight through him, the other two had lodged in his body. It was these that had to be located in the dim light of dawn, under a copper lamp. The doctor was short of instruments and short of time; they'd arrived too late as it was. By the time they finished, it was nine o'clock. Dr. Gyarmathy came out into the yard and looked taken aback as if he'd only just realised that there were people sitting and waiting by the wall.

'Go home, all of you. Go,' he said and wanted to add, as he usually did, that everything would be fine, but he didn't, because he didn't believe that himself.

'Shouldn't we tell his mother?' asked one of the women, but the doctor just waved her away and ushered them out of his yard.

After the operation my father ran a temperature; the doctor said it was a miracle he didn't die of sepsis. They took him over to Dr. Gyarmathy's sisters, where he lay – as a 'relative' – for three weeks, all the while his mother thought he'd fled to Budapest and was ready to *wring his neck the moment he showed his face*.

Now in his tenth decade, Dr. Gyarmathy had no memory of the documents he'd filled out afterwards. Even the name meant nothing to him: there must be some mistake, he kept assuring my mother as he showed her out, it was all so long ago. He'd help if he could, he really would. Then, as he opened the gate, he suddenly looked at my mother again and said: 'I'm sorry. I'm frightened.' Then he closed the gate.

So, the documents about the car accident never turned up, but with a strict diet a further operation could – for the time being, they said – be avoided. My father pottered about at home, forbidden to do any heavy lifting, but as the weeks went by, he found doing nothing harder and harder to bear. He sat in front of the television all day long, watching the borders being strengthened. Hour after hour they showed footage of the fanatical, stone-throwing foreigners storming the border fence. He nodded in approval: *a good thing, that fence. It'll protect us. Whoever came up with it had the right idea.* He was especially impressed by the barbed wire. He decided to have his own fence repaired too and protect his property. Not just because the dog was constantly barking and bothering the pedestrians – with my mother in constant dread that they'd give it rat-poison because of the noise it made – but also because of the litter left by the yobs hanging around the off-licence, the empty bottles and food wrappers they threw into our front garden. He was fired up by the thought that he'd get things sorted out properly at last. And anyway, he would add, no reason for everyone to stare into our backyard, it's not a cinema. What he had in mind was a high fence, solid stone, with six-inch nails on top.

My mother was against the idea: it would turn the house into a fortress. But my father was adamant. He was so excited by all the planning and the preparations that he more or less forgot about his illness and his medications. He felt invigorated, a young man again.

They totted up the figures: the fence cost a fortune. More than my father was counting on and more than he could afford. But he dug his heels in. That was the kind of fence he wanted, and that was that. None of anyone one else's business.

He talked things over with the workmen; they strode around purposefully, took measurements, and he never mentioned the cost again, as if it didn't matter.

Just make sure it's good and strong, he would keep saying, which really infuriated my mother: why did a bloody fence have to be so damn strong, who'd be coming here with a tank, she'd say, but my father said nothing and stuck to his guns. He waved my mother away: really not something she should stick her oar into.

When the stonemasons came, he opened out both wings

of the wire-mesh gate to let them in. There were four of them, on a small truck with a cement mixer and shovels and sacks. My father did think it odd that the dog didn't bark at them, but he put it to the back of his mind. He helped carry the tools and hump the smaller sacks, as if he'd forgotten on purpose about everything he wasn't allowed to do. He told the men to mind the grass and do their mixing only at the back, circling round with the wheelbarrow, and showed them where to ditch the dirty water. 'And in case it rains the tools could be put in here,' he said, opening the green garage door, which had streaks of blood in front of it. The dog lay inside.

'And what's this here?' asked one of the men.

My father stared numbly.

'It's done for,' he said quietly, as if trying to explain to himself what he was seeing, totally at a loss, as if not even wanting to check whether it was still warm, as if he didn't want to rush off with it somewhere, to do something, anything, as if he'd never seen it before, as if it weren't even his – ours – as if he hadn't that very morning stroked that now completely lifeless, little body.

'It's done for,' he repeated, as if passing sentence over it, then rubbed his face vigorously and went off to tell the men what to do next. On his way he stepped into the trail of blood.

'We had one too,' one of the men offered. 'Kept dashing off, till it got run over by a car.'

My father looked him up and down but said nothing. He turned away and hurried off to show them where to dump the sand.

Reunited

Muyesser Abdul'ehed

Translated from the Uyghur by Munawwar Abdulla

'HE HIT ME. HE hit my head. The police should arrest him, too!' he says to himself. The police. He becomes afraid again. 'The police don't arrest the bad guys. The police shouldn't take him, but he should be punished.'

The blood trickling down from the wound on his head mixes with his tears and paints his face crimson. He keeps on walking.

People pass by and look like they recognise him. One lady asks him whose child he is. He says nothing. He pushes her aside and keeps going. Would she have taken him to his parents? No! She'd just have taken him to that place again. And that dorm is so cold that it's no different to being outside. So, so what if he stays out? He's going to find his parents. He is! He becomes sad again. The smell of polo hits him, and he remembers the one his mother used to make.

He had come home from school, and the delicious aroma of polo had wafted towards him.

'Mum!' He ran in and hugged her. She was cooking in the outside kitchen that they used in summer.

'My darling lamb, are you hungry? Look,' she said, nodding at the stove, 'I'm cooking your favourite polo. I just need to braise it a little longer and it'll be ready.' She looked at him. 'Oh my, why are your clothes so dirty? You must have been wrestling with the other children again. Alright, go wash and change. The food will be done soon, and your dad will probably be back by then.'

The handlebars of a man's bike appeared in the doorway, rattling the gate. In its basket was a bag of apples.

'Dad!' he ran to his father now, forgetting his mother.

'Look at him,' she said, laughing. 'He sees the apples and forgets the polo! He sees his dad and forgets his mum!'

The three of them sat eating polo in the chaykhana. Three of the apples his father had brought home had been pressed into the rice and meat. He'd really loved those apples.

An apple stalk pokes out through the snow. He hesitates for a moment, then carefully pulls on the stalk. The apple is half-eaten. His vision dims, his head hurts. He looks around his wide, empty surroundings and sees no one. Just white. He wipes the uneaten side of the apple on the snow and bites into it, bit by bit. It is an Aport apple, the same kind his dad had brought home.

'We don't have these kinds of apples in our yard, Dad. We should plant some.'

'Sure! But we don't plant apples. When spring comes, I'll bring home an apple sapling, and you can grow it yourself.'

But the spring his dad spoke of never came. Well, spring came, but it wasn't one his dad was in.

He carries on eating the frozen apple. He looks at it in his hand and thinks about the tree he was supposed to grow. It's definitely going to be a huge tree, with lots of branches. One day he will suddenly notice it blossoming, and it will start to fruit, and when the apples ripen just a little he'll taste them and his mum will say, 'Hey, son, eat it when it's fully ripe or you'll upset your stomach.' But his dad won't get too mad – he probably ate a lot of unripe fruit when he was a kid. And when these apples do ripen fully, he bets they will be so sweet. And then his mum will press them into the polo. He only realises that he'd sunk into this daydream when his tears begin to swell and roll coldly down his face, over where the last lot had dried.

The half-eaten apple is lasting longer than he'd expected. So, this is what it means when they say teng yégen ten'ge singer. But now he becomes fixed in his place, as though all his nerves have stopped functioning and he is far away from his earthly senses, his lips blue with cold, his teeth chattering, his stomach squirming in pain from the frosty apple he's put in it. Somehow, though, a force pushes him forward. Because he has to find his parents. He cannot stop.

If his parents knew that his teacher had hit his head, he thinks, then they'd definitely get him to pay. He's so cruel. He had hit his hands so hard that he couldn't do his homework. And then he'd hit his head because he hadn't done the work. All they feed them in school is cabbage soup and rice, and the hard bread they get with tea twice a day. He'll tell his parents all of this, and they'll definitely take him out of that school and put him in a good one. A faint smile makes its way to his shivering lips.

He'd really loved the first school he'd gone to. That year, Sister Tursunay from his neighbourhood was taking a new batch of students. Before he joined, she'd say playfully to him, 'I'm going to teach you!' And that's exactly what he wanted, as he stubbornly told his parents.

His mother laughed, and his father teased him: 'Well no

one could teach you other than Sister Tursunay, anyway. You don't listen to anyone else.'

And so it was: 'Oh, is my little brother grown up enough to study now? Come, you'll be in my class,' Sister Tursunay told him. Sister Tursunay became Ms Tursunay, and she would pick him up in the morning and bring him home from school in the evening. On the journey back she'd ask him questions about what he'd learned. She quickly became his favourite teacher.

But what he learned, at the age of seven, was that good days never stretch for long for those who are unlucky.

'Did your teacher tell you that you can learn other languages better when you excel in your own language?' the strangers asked him.

'Yes, she did! Our teacher gives us brilliant lessons.' For that one 'yes', he was to be forever separated from Ms Tursunay. And the peculiar sniggers of those complete strangers in the Principal's office are replayed in his mind to this day, again and again, like a fearful judgement from far away.

'A different teacher taught us today,' he told his mother. 'He said we wouldn't be learning Uyghur from now on, and that we shouldn't talk in Uyghur at home, and that the national language is something called our "mother tongue" now.' He paused and then looked at his mother. 'Mum, where did Ms Tursunay go?'

She was silent. And then she suddenly hugged him and sobbed.

One day, a boy whispered in his ear, 'You snitched on Ms Tursunay, that's why they took her away.'

'No! I didn't snitch! Who said that?' he shouted back.

He was punished for shouting in Uyghur, that day. When everyone left, he was made to sweep his class three times and then to wipe down the floors.

'I snitched on Ms. Tursunay. I was the one who said "yes".

The police should take me as well.' The thought was imprinted in him from then on.

The apple in his hand feels like it is getting bigger. Who had eaten half of it and then thrown it away? Maybe some spoilt child. What if, he thinks suddenly, trembling, it was a Chinese person? What would happen if he ate something one of them had bitten into? 'Your mind will be corrupted,' his mother would say. He looks at the apple with blurry eyes, and then tosses it away reluctantly.

Now they'll take me away too, he thought.

The sound of sirens reached him. The police, with their rifles on their belts and handguns in their hands, stormed into the house.

'All of you, kneel down and raise your hands above your heads!'

They never kneeled down to people.

The police began to hit his mother and father with their batons. He stood nervously in a corner, watching on. And then he came suddenly to his senses, shouting 'Mum!' as he threw himself at her. The policeman, his face covered in black cloth, pulled them apart and shook him aggressively until he was still. The house was searched and the important books that his mother had bundled together were thrown into the middle of the yard. By the time he got to the front gate, the police car was already far away, with his parents in it.

My parents are in the police car.

With his broken Chinese, he asked his teacher the next day, 'What can we do to get into a police car?'

Dismayed by the question, his teacher said, as if to scare him, 'If you don't listen to your teacher, or if you don't obey the school rules, then the police will come and take you away.' And so from then on he didn't listen, and he broke what rules he could break, and he started coming to school later and later. Each day, he would be reprimanded and beaten by the teacher. But the police didn't appear. The days passed agonisingly slowly. He would sit at home on his own, his neighbours and relatives occasionally checking in on him, listening and waiting for the sirens.

Finally, the police car came back. He didn't get scared this time. No – he was happy. But when they put him in the car, however much he searched, he couldn't see his parents.

'Where are my parents?' he asked.

'Quiet.'

As they drove, he sat back, knowing that they would soon arrive to his parents, enjoying the journey that would take him to them. But he didn't see them when they arrived. What he saw were walls, a place surrounded by walls, where a cold-looking official received them in a building and wrote something on a piece of paper. He was passed on to a woman who looked even colder, the police officers still escorting him.

And at this point he managed to speak up. 'I want to see my parents.'

'What's he saying?' the woman asked in Chinese.

One of the officers interpreted for her.

'Your mother and father are not here,' she said angrily. 'They did the wrong thing. They were detained.' She jabbed her hand onto the table in front of her repeatedly as she spoke. 'You will be educated to become a good person. Otherwise, you will face the consequences like your parents.' Seeing the blank expression on his face, she told the officer to translate. His tone was slightly softer, his eyes slightly more caring, a bit like his dad's. But the officer looked afraid as he spoke. And his dad was never afraid.

He knew for sure, then, that he wouldn't find his parents in the police car, or in that walled building, and for the first time tears welled in his eyes.

He keeps on walking. He hasn't let go of the hope that his parents will show up. Something inside him had started him on this path, and his parents will definitely be at the end of this road. If he believes anything, he believes this.

They didn't look for him. But they maybe did, actually, and probably just couldn't find him because he wasn't at home. It would be good if he went home and had a look. But if he goes home, he'll get caught. And if he gets caught, they will take him back to that place.

His face goes from red to blue, his feet freeze, out to the tips of his toes, and he finally loses all feeling in them.

Maybe they were detained. Maybe they took them the same way they took him. Right – otherwise they would have definitely looked for him.

He thinks of the song his mother used to sing.

My dear child Qembernisa,
Your fire is strong Meremnisa,
My dear child Qembernisa,
Your fire is strong Meremnisa.

This song always seemed so funny to him. But when she sang it, she would cry. She told him it was composed by a mother who had been separated from her two daughters. Was his mother thinking, back then, about her own parents who she'd left far away in Atush? Or about the daughter who'd died before him?

Of course! he thought. Of course he'll be able to save them. He managed to run away from school, didn't he? He became suddenly very proud of himself. If his parents were to hear about this, they would definitely be proud too. His dad would say, 'That's my boy!' And his mum would purse her lips and say, 'My my, when he does something good, he's your boy, but when he does something bad, suddenly he's mine, hey?'

83

He can't feel his feet, but they keep on walking him forwards.

He could help them escape. He could hide them in the back of a car that had driven into wherever they were being held. Then, when the car left and stopped at a gas station, they could run away together, when no one was looking. No one would spot them, that way – just as no one had spotted him when he'd escaped with the same plan.

One time he went off to the river with his friends without telling anyone. When he returned home, drenched head to toe, he was greeted by the sight of his mother wailing and his father pacing up and down the house.

'Where did you go?' The words exploded out of his father's mouth as soon as he set eyes on him.

His mother stepped in front of his father. 'Oh, my dear son,' she said, hugging him. 'He's come back safe and sound. No need to scare him.'

He promised his father that he would never do it again. It had frightened him, seeing his parents like that. His father has never hit him, but he believes that he might have done, that day, if his mother hadn't got in the way.

Where should they go once he's saved his parents? If they go to his grandmother's in Atush, no one will be able to find them. Mum said Atush was really far away, and it was so difficult to get there when they went last year. The police definitely won't be able to go there. He is intoxicated with thoughts of his heroism. His grandmother will call him her hero boy and sit him right at the head of the table. Wait – he can't go to the head of the table, the elders should sit there. Mum and dad can sit there. Even though he saved them, they are older than him.

His stomach begins to rumble and he regrets, a little, throwing the apple away.

Stomach, not now. Could it not wait until they get to Atush to feel hungry? His grandmother will make amazing food. She'll definitely make some narin.

He'd fallen in love with the narin he ate in Atush. His mother had made it before, but his grandmother's was even more delicious.

Should he eat polo first, or narin? He should certainly eat little by little, otherwise his stomach will hurt, and he won't be able to eat it all. Last year, he ate so much of his grandmother's food that his stomach got bloated and sore, and his grandmother had to concoct some medicine to make him better.

He licks his lips. It's as if a tablecloth with all those foods has been set up right on the thick snow in front of him. He walks slowly towards it, reaches out, and grabs a handful of what to him looks like polo. His grandmother says it is tastier to eat polo with your hands.

What sort of cold polo is this? He wonders if it's been a while since it was cooked? He feels a little bit annoyed. His grandmother never gives leftovers to guests. And he is no ordinary guest, either: he is a hero, a guest of honour, isn't he?

But his stomach has stopped grumbling, and so he stops thinking about the cold polo and starts walking forwards again. It's a good thing that just a handful of that polo had filled him up. He doesn't want to eat any more of it. It's too cold.

After walking for a while, he realises that the roads look familiar. He stops and looks around. But there is nothing but a white expanse, dotted with trees covered in more white.

Then he thinks he sees two profiles in the distance. A laugh that had disappeared for the last two months bubbles up to his face. He recognises his mother's woollen scarf, her down jacket. She is stamping her heeled boots into the snow and walking forwards. Next to her is the winter hat that matches the one he bought with his dad, and his father's familiar black overcoat. If the snow weren't there, he'd spin around and dance. He wants to run, but he can't in this snow. And then even walking becomes difficult, his legs becoming ice.

'Mum!' He screams with all the power he has left. 'Dad!' His voice spreads out around him, but they don't seem to hear. He wills himself into walking forwards, his eyes glued to his parents. The blood has stopped dripping from his head and has dried and frozen on his face.

He finally found them! And they're definitely walking towards Atush. But he didn't actually save them, so his grandmother won't ask him to sit at the head of the table, he supposes. But that's OK. He wasn't going to sit there anyway.

He feels a little crestfallen about no longer being a hero, but it is overcome by the excitement of finding his parents. But why can't they hear him? Or are they talking to each other and not noticing? Or do they think he's some other kid? Now he feels himself become grumpy – they hadn't looked for him, even though they'd managed to escape from the police car. Are they looking for him? He stops and thinks. No! If they were looking for him, they wouldn't be going this way. This is definitely the way to Atush. Ah! But, if they realised that he would be going to Atush? Then that's different. He will still ask them when he reaches them: 'Why didn't you look for me?' He will sulk a little, but when they explain why he will understand, like a grown-up.

'Polo with apples...'

'My mum's hand...'

'Dad, hug me tight...'

His tongue seems to be freezing now, too. And his brain even. He must still be walking, though. Stars appear in front of him, and begin to increase in number. One leg is plunging into an endless emptiness. It feels like night is falling. It feels like the night is wrapping him up in darkness, refusing to show the full moon's pockmarked face. The stars – the magic of the stars that he used to count on summer nights in the courtyard. The starts that seemed so close when he looked at them, and yet were so far away when he wanted to reach them. The stars whose playful twinkling was so familiar with him. He smiles. His hand is just about to reach his parents. 'Mum! Dad! I'm back. From now on I won't leave the house without telling you.' He's sinking into a sweet slumber in his parents embrace. He descends further down, the muscles in his arms and legs cramping in the ice. He closes his eyes. He'll keep them shut. Now nothing, no one, can separate them again, not even the police car.

Brandy Sour

Constantia Soteriou

Translated from the Greek by Lina Protopapa

Brandy Sour: The King

THEY SAY THAT A barman invented the cocktail for King Farouk of Egypt in the 1940s – a dark time for the king, by then no longer the handsome, athletic boy charming Europe with his Western manners, but a heavy, middle-aged man faced with all kinds of troubles and political headaches, who had to conceal his fondness for alcohol. They say that he had come to Cyprus for a break after a trip to England; that he stayed in Platres, the most cosmopolitan village on the island; and that he lodged in the only hotel that could possibly host him, The Forest Park. They say that, in the evening, he had left his attendants in the room, that he'd had a rough day, that he had previously met with the English governor of the island, that they had argued, and that Farouk was tired. They say that he had sat at the hotel bar alone and that he had asked the barman to fix him something. 'Fix me something,' said Farouk to the barman. 'Fix me something that doesn't look like a drink, something that looks like it doesn't contain any alcohol, something with a bit of that good cognac of yours that I like so much – oh, and add some lemon, too. I like your lemons.'

It's true what he said about our lemons: we have good lemons.

The man behind the bar listened to Farouk sympathetically and poured all his mastery into a drink worthy of kings who want to deceive people: he added cognac to help the king forget and lemonade for sweetness, but also sour lemons to remind the king of his sorrows and Angostura bitters to heighten the bitterness, and he poured it all in a highball glass, and the drink looked very much like an iced tea. 'Here you go!' Before you fill the glass with all the ingredients, you must first sugar its rim and, finally, you must top it all off with a sweet little cherry. A maraschino cherry. It's a good drink, brandy sour. They say that King Farouk liked it a lot. It's a Cypriot drink with Cypriot ingredients that you serve in a tall, sugar-rimmed glass – a drink full of cognac and lemonade that seems and tastes innocent, but is not. It's a drink worthy of kings who want to deceive people, a drink that isn't what it seems to be. It looks like iced tea and you can drink it publicly without anyone knowing that it isn't. It's a drink full of secrets – that's why it was made here. Cognac, lemons, and Angostura for bitterness – you can't have a brandy sour without the bitterness.

Brandy Sour:
1 part cognac
2–3 drops of Angostura bitters
Lemonade
Sour lemons
Soda water
Decorate with a slice of lemon and a glazed cherry on
a toothpick, and offer to the king.

***

Lavender Tea: The Jew

The nightingales wake him up. Whatever the weather, he always leaves the window slightly open so that he can hear them. The singing of the birds and the cool air remind him of Zurich and Germany. Then he drinks the hot lavender tea that the young maid leaves for him on the bedside table and goes for a walk up in the mountains. He knows that the villagers find his mountain walks odd. In a village where everyone is a labourer or a farmer, it is strange to see somebody so eagerly seek physical exercise and the weariness that comes with it. Nevertheless, they greet him on their way to work. 'Good morning, Mr. Architect. Enjoy your walk, Mr. Benzion.' They are open-hearted people, simple and friendly, and they insist on offering him figs and other delicacies. He declines the gifts – all of them except the lavender bunches, which he hands over to the maid who prepares his hot lavender tea in the morning. It's wonderful, this tea. So typical of the village, so aromatic and delightful. He didn't know you could drink lavender; he didn't know you could eat it, either. His mother would freshen her clothes and her linen with it. Mother, lavender, Zurich, Germany, the cold. 'Good morning, Mr. Benzion. Enjoy your walk, Mr. Architect.' His mother, her lavender, his Zurich, their Germany, the cold.

He thinks about all of this over and over as he walks in the morning. Or perhaps he walks and walks so that he might forget all of this. Nobody in the village knows how he ended up on the island after the war – or when, exactly – nor do they know why he is so highly sought-after. No house, no building, no hotel is constructed without him being involved somehow: he seems to be a part of everything, and everyone wants his advice. 'Let's get Mr. Benzion's opinion,' everyone says. Nobody knows much else about him: who he really is, where his loved ones are, if he likes spending all his time here, if he enjoys what he does. All they know is that he demands a good pay – 'He is a Jew after all,' they say, repeating the slurs they have heard, as though he weren't the first Jew they had ever met – that he dislikes the heat and drinking alcohol – he loathes alcohol – and that he always speaks slowly and softly, with his hands in the pockets of his black jacket. He only ever wears black, and his English is inflected with a heavy German accent. And he doesn't say much, either. He's a man of few words. 'He talks like a man who knows fear or who has once known fear' – that's what the village priest once said about him. 'He talks like a man who loves walls more than he loves other people.' That kind of man. A man who loves walls only, stones only, buildings only. His mother, her lavender, his Zurich, their Germany, the cold. That's the kind of man he is.

Everyone on the island – the English governors and the local bourgeoisie too – respects him. Perhaps they are even a little intimidated by him. He doesn't feel at ease with anyone, but he does feel a slight affinity for the simple villagers who offer him their lavender. After all, he did not come here to make friends; he came here to build houses. He is a man who loves walls. His first building was a cinema theatre in Limassol, a building with sharp lines, austere, just like him. That's the building Skyrianides, a rich merchant from the village, sees, and that's why he asks him to oversee the construction of his new hotel, The Forest Park. Many more will follow. Anyone who's anyone in the city wants a house designed by 'Mr. Benzion, the Architect, the Jew.' As long as they can afford it. And as long as they can convince him. They say he isn't too adamant about keeping to his sharp Zurich lines either, that he is willing to accommodate the owners' wishes, that he is willing to build them the houses they want. If anyone knew him better, they would think that he likes to make people happy. But nobody knows him.

For a few years, he goes back and forth between Jaffa, Limassol, and Platres. His cold. Jaffa is too warm for his taste – too warm to bear, really. And there is a lot that he can no longer bear. Platres. His cold. At times, he thinks he could even stay here forever. Here in the village, with the nightingales waking him up in the morning. He could stay here forever if he wanted to. 'You could, if you wanted. You could stay here forever,' the maid tells him as she leaves his bed in the morning to prepare their lavender tea. It's superb, this tea: so aromatic and so delightful. He had no idea that lavender was something you could drink, that it was something you could eat. He had no idea that he could consider staying here forever. His cold.

It's never cold in Nicosia. The city is a boiling pit in the summer. It's a lot like Jaffa, only with a river, the Pedieos, and with enough space for a new hotel. 'This is something only you could design, something only you could execute successfully,' Skyrianides tells him. He offers him iced lavender tea with honey in a tall glass filled to the brim with ice. He had no idea that you could also have this tea iced, and he had no idea that he, and only he, could build this new gem of a hotel, the most exquisite hotel in the whole of the Middle East and the whole of the Mediterranean too. Skyrianides gives him full permission to build the walls of his dreams, as long as there is something of the island about them, something of its stones, something of its colours and its tradition. 'Something of the island's heat,' he tells him, 'something of its cold.' He could stay here forever, here in the village. He had no idea you could drink lavender, no idea you could eat it, no idea at all. But, instead, at the break of dawn, he leaves for the Bellapais Abbey. He strolls around the monastery's courtyard for days, studying the building. If you were to look at the new hotel on the banks of the river, you would easily make out the architectural affinity to the monastery: in the yellow sandstone that is so typical of the buildings all over the island, in the pointed arches, in the antefixes. The hotel comprises three floors; 93 rooms, each with its own bathroom and telephone; a dining room; a ballroom; and 1,350 electric light bulbs that light it up. Seen from a distance, the pointed arches in the portico, at the entrance, and the façade, together with the tall windows, resemble lavender flowers.

> *Lavender Tea:*
> A bunch of dried lavender flowers
> Very hot water
> Infuse dried flowers in hot water
> Strain
> Add honey, if you wish
> Helps you forget.

★★★

Commandaria: The Maid

Of all the foreigners she came across in the hotel, the one she will always remember is Yuri Gagarin. Not Princess Margaret, not Aliki Vougiouklaki – with whom everyone was in love – not even Elizabeth Taylor. She will remember Yuri Gagarin because he once left the earth and rose to the heavens and saw the moon from up close. Of course, when she goes up to the village to visit her family, those few days when she takes her leave, the people there are more interested in hearing about the hotel and its great luxuries. Nobody can fathom that each room has its very own bathroom and its very own tap with hot and cold water where the foreigners can bathe whenever they want – even every day, if they wish – and a ballroom and a hairdresser and a tennis court. 'What's a tennis?' Everyone wants to hear about the Venetian room, the large ballroom with its oak hardwood floors and its Italian chandeliers and its Greek marble. And the balls: the beautiful gowns the women wear, the elaborate hairdos, the food. So far, nobody has asked her about Gagarin. Nobody cares if he had travelled from the earth all the way to the stars. Of all the guests she encountered in the hotel, she will always remember Yuri: his pale face, his slender hands, how minute he looked and how much he liked Commandaria. In a tall glass with lots of ice, enough ice to water it down. Gagarin's Commandaria reminded her nothing of the holy communion that the village priest offered them, the sacramental wine in the small spoon, the take-eat-drink-ye-all of it – no, Gagarin's Commandaria reminded her nothing of God, and the only thing she regrets is not having asked, not having found a way to ask him, if, when he had travelled all the way up to the stars, he had managed to see God.

Commandaria:
Highball glass
Lots of ice
For cosmonauts and all those who want to see God.

***

VSOP Brandy: The Guerrilla Fighter

The people who frequent the hotel's lounges love their brandy: they pour it in capacious glasses that look like tulips, and they serve it slightly cold, just cold enough that it reaches room temperature by the time it's in the hands of the gentleman who will consume it, so that it can then rise to his body temperature. The ladies never take their brandy straight; when they do have some, it's as an addition to a cocktail in a long-stemmed glass. The local ladies and the English ladies alike have a predilection for cocktails containing brandy served in long-stemmed glasses. The guerrilla fighters up in the mountains drink it straight out of the bottle. The ladies and the gentlemen, be they locals or English, prefer the VSOP brandy. Up in the mountains, when they send Demetris to shop for supplies, he goes for KEO. It has a bitter almond aftertaste that he likes. We never use KEO for brandy sours. We only use VSOP. Demetris has never had a brandy sour, but he hears that the people at the hotel love it. He confirms this soon enough, when he starts working as a waiter at the bar there, serving drinks to the English and the others – the locals. He wears dark trousers with a crease, a perfectly ironed white shirt, and well-polished shoes. The maître, who is the person in charge of the staff, is very strict and won't allow him to use brilliantine on his hair: 'This is a serious hotel. We have standards here.' The English seem to feel very much at home in the serious hotel: they laugh a lot and they let go, they unbutton their shirts a little, they make jokes about the heat and about the indigenous people – not the locals who rub shoulders with them at the hotel, the other ones, the ones who live in the villages. It's the first time Demetris has worked as a waiter, and he likes it. He hears the beautifully spoken Greek in the lobby and also some Turkish and lots of English, too. He serves drinks to the English and he gathers information that he then passes on to his captain. It's a serious hotel. The English seem to feel at home: they laugh a lot and they let go and they joke about the heat and other things, too – things that they shouldn't joke about – and Demetris passes everything on to the guerrillas up in the mountains. The English here are nothing like the English he sees on the streets. They wear their uniforms loosely and they laugh out loud, and they offer Demetris cigarettes, and they give him conspiratorial pats on the back, and they sometimes bring him magazines with shameless naked women who seem to laugh out loud jubilantly. They like KEO brandy too and they ostentatiously ignore brandy sours. Demetris looks at them and laughs. He has recently got very close to a Johnny and a Bryan. One evening, after his shift, the three of them sit out in the garden with the jasmines and Bryan shows Demetris some photos of his girlfriend, Jane, and his dog, Ruth, back at home, and they drink brandy straight out of the bottle. One day, just before the annual ball of the Caledonian Society, where all the island's high society gathers – ladies, gentlemen, locals and English – Demetris installs a homemade bomb in the ballroom. Four people are injured – a maid and three Englishmen – none of them seriously. He is, in any case, arrested and locked up in the English jail, which is a pity, because he will never be able to work in the hotel again and, as a consequence, he will miss Adamantios Diamantis's painting exhibition, which is the talk of the town in 1957, as well as the luncheon served in the ballroom by the last governor of the island, where Makarios and Fazıl Küçük will also be present. On the menu will be celery consommé, lobster Parisienne, fondant potatoes, seasonal vegetables, salade grecque and Peach Melba. He would later find out that they did not offer any brandy in the end. No brandy at the end of the meal.

VSOP Brandy:
Brandy glass
Room temperature
Can also be drunk straight out of the bottle.

★★★

Ayran: The Turk

Every day, he takes the shortcut from King Edward VII Street and walks past the big Greek hotel to go to work, and every day, he buys his ayran from Mr. Alexian, who is on a little street nearby. Not everyone knows how to make a good ayran: you need the right kind of milk – goat's milk – to make yoghurt with, and then you need to add more milk to the yoghurt and whisk it all well. Finally, you need to add salt and lots of mint. Mr. Alexian knows his ayran: he's Armenian. In Turkey, where he had been, they made their ayran with lots of salt and no mint but, as his grandmother used to say, you can't have ayran without mint. Best not to have it at all if there's no mint in it. Sometimes, he thinks that the reason he likes this drink so much is because it reminds him of his grandmother – so much so that he can put up with the bewildered stares he gets from his compatriots and from the hotel valet, too, as he walks by. One day, somebody from the Greek side comes up to him and asks: 'Where is it you go every morning and why do you have to always walk past here?' A few days after the question, the street in front of the big hotel – once named after the British king – is renamed Markou Drakou, after the man who had just recently become a national hero. And then, one morning, he sees people installing sandbags there, and with his poor Greek he gathers that this is a measure taken in order to protect hotel guests from potential Turkish-Cypriot fire. For an entire month, he can't go through at all, and until the UN remove the sandbags from the area, he can't buy his ayran. When he had attempted to pass through, they stopped him and told him he needed to go back. He needs to find another way to work, another way to go get his ayran, another place to buy it from – or maybe he needs to stop drinking it altogether. In a few days, everything will change. He'll manage to sneak to Mr. Alexian's just once more, for one last ayran. It's

Mr. Alexian who tells him that it's not a good idea for him to walk past the big hotel any more. Mr. Alexian says that this whole situation frightens him a lot, and he offers him his last ayran – this one is on him. He adds lots of salt and lots of mint, too. Best not to drink ayran at all, if it doesn't have lots of mint in it. In a few days, everything will change: he will need to find a new way to work, or perhaps he will need to change jobs altogether, and maybe he'll need to stop drinking this drink that his grandmother loved so much. In the end, he finds a job as an assistant in his uncle's law firm in the old city centre, close to the Saray Hotel. It's their hotel, the Turkish one, grand and luxurious, like the hotel the others have 'on their side,' as his uncle says while they drink their coffee – it's coffee, now – in the morning. 'Each to their own home, their own side, their own hotel – isn't it better to have coffee in the morning instead of that atrocious ayran?'

Ayran:
Yoghurt
Cold goat's milk
Whisk well
Add mint and a bit of salt
Best not to drink the ayran at all if it has no mint.

★★★

Water: The Mother

She is awoken by the sound of shots being fired, but she doesn't realise this immediately. She initially thinks it's a headache that wakes her up; she thinks she must have spent too much time in the sun the previous day and that – this is more likely – the two cocktails she'd had in order to tolerate another day at the pool with the kids must not have been such a brilliant idea. She'd give anything for an ice-cold glass of water right now. Tommy was spending yet another day covering the latest events. Some holiday, this was. And to add insult to injury, he wouldn't let her take the kids and go to a pension in Kyrenia. 'Best to stay in Nicosia. Best we all stick together.' Some holiday. The ache hammers relentlessly inside her head. Boom boom boom boom boom. But it's footsteps and knocking she's hearing outside the door now. 'Madam, get dressed, take the children, and go to the basement. The war just broke out.' Where is Tommy? Tommy? She would give anything right now for a big glass of ice-cold water. She needs to grab the children, they need to put on their shoes – quick, to the basement. She grabs a blanket, the kids, her glasses – she forgets the water. In the basement of the hotel are women, children crying, people screaming; her children won't let go of her skirt. They sit among other women and children, and they wait. Above them, they hear bullets raging, they hear whistles and voices. Some holiday, eh? Truly. She is thirsty. She would give anything for a big glass of ice-cold water. Tommy had told her that the hotel was built on a river. She hugs her children and tells them stories about rivers and water and waterfalls. Her children hold on to her skirt, tight. She reassures the other women that they are safe; she tells them that everything will be OK, that they are not in danger, that they are safe in the basement. They are foreigners, they won't let anyone harm them. Above their heads, the hotel is caught up in a bullet storm. Makarios doesn't want the Turks to have it. There are screams, explosions, trampling. She would give anything for a big glass of icy-cold water. 'Madam, get dressed and get the children, go to the basement, there's a war.' There's a hammering pain in her head. They will later find out that the hotel was struck by two enormous mortar shells. She doesn't sleep at all that night; she counts the hours with the pounding in her head. She would give anything for a big, huge glass of ice-cold water. The children hold on to her tight by her skirt even as they sleep. At the break of dawn, the doors open, and a maid descends to the basement with a limp. She is followed by the UN soldiers who will lead them to the UN vehicles. They are escorted by a UN convoy under Canadian command.

Once they are on the lorry bed, the UN soldiers offer everyone a drink of water from their water flasks – warm water, almost salty. Tommy had told her that the hotel was built on a river. She would give anything for a big glass of ice-cold water right now. They are all transported to the airport. The children hold on to her tight by her skirt as she flies back home. Tommy will reach them later on, in September, after he has covered everything about the war. Since then, she has carried this thirst with her every summer. She's always thirsty in July. She gives anything, everything, for a big glass of ice-cold water.

Water:
In a big glass, ice-cold
Sometimes you have to give everything for a big glass
of water.

***

Coffee: The Maître

He wakes up at dawn and he goes to the kitchen to have his coffee prepared just the way he likes it. It's the only cup of coffee he will have the whole day. With lots of kaymak and no sugar. Turkish coffee – 'Greek' coffee, he always has to correct himself – with sugar is an absolute waste of coffee. It needs to be bitter – there's no other way to drink it. Coffee time is the one moment of the day when he gets to relax. He takes it outside, in the garden with the jasmines, before the hotel guests wake up, before the day begins. Only after he has had his coffee can the day begin. He manages the staff with an iron fist in a velvet glove and everything that happens does so under his supervision. The Skyrianides family had him trained in Venice. Nothing is done in the hotel without his approval: from the waiters' uniforms to the next day's menu. After all, he is the one who compiles the hotel's employee manual, which contains all the relevant rules and regulations. Whenever there are receptions and balls at the hotel, he is in his element, organising, talking to the people in charge, giving advice on everything from the menu to the flower arrangements. Everyone knows him and everyone knows that he is the one to call on in case of an emergency – the maître. He is the reason for the great success of 'Elegance', the fashion show organised by the French committee; of the ball of the Medical Society of Nicosia; of the balls of the Caledonian Society; and of the art exhibitions that are the main topic of conversation among high society. He knows the hotel to the last detail: every corner, every chair, every tiny little piece of it. If it didn't sound so trite, one would say the hotel is like his own child. Everyone who knows him knows that he is the person to call on in case of an emergency. When the shooting starts, his first concern is to help protect the foreign customers; he is the one who takes the initiative to have them hide in the basement and then to escape under UN supervision. As the fighting rages and the bullets strike the hotel mercilessly, he feels as though the bullets are penetrating his body. He will never recover from the shell fire. When the hotel is ordered to evacuate and eventually ends up in the hands of the UN, he is the one who will instruct the hotel staff how to safeguard the furniture and the silverware. When he packs his suitcase and is forced to leave, he feels like he's taking everything that the hotel had ever been with him. Back at home now, he anxiously follows the negotiations about the Cyprus problem on the TV so that he can steal a glimpse or two of the hotel, so that he can get an idea of the state of the rooms and the yards. The first thing he notices is that somebody must have pulled out the weeds in a fury. He will later learn that they had died, and that somebody had planted some cactuses in their place. In every TV frame, he catches glimpses of his beloved Venetian room falling apart: the walls cracked, the flooring ruined, water leaking everywhere. All the while, the leaders of the Greeks and the Turks continue to meet at the hotel regularly. At some point he finds out that the big ballroom has become a lunch spot for the Argentinian Blue Helmets who sit on plastic chairs there or in the cactus garden, not having coffee but drinking mate instead. Sometimes, he arranges to meet with former colleagues in an old coffee shop downtown. He's taken to drinking coffee in the afternoons, too, nowadays – no sugar, the way people take their coffee at funerals, the way people take their coffee in grief and in tragedy and in death. That kind of coffee. He takes his coffee with thick kaymak and no sugar. Coffee needs to be bitter, there's no other way about it.

Coffee (Turkish, Greek, Cypriot):
Water
Boil on hot embers
It needs to be bitter – no other way about it.

***

Rose Water: The Daughter

Her mother uses it everywhere: in food, in drinks, on her face. Best not even to leave the house if you don't sprinkle some rose water on your face first. It refreshes, it tones, and it cauterises wounds. Her mother puts it everywhere — not just in deserts: she adds it to the food she cooks, she sprinkles it on her head, her face, her eyes, her bosom too. 'That's what I want you to pour over my grave,' she says. 'Rose water: sprinkle it on my cross, pour it over the soil to keep me fresh.' Her mum makes it to the other side before the war, a few months before the summer. She dies, and the rest of them flee with nothing — nothing, not even the rose water — and the grave is left to dry up for thirty or so years. Nobody is there to pour anything over it. When the checkpoints open and everyone is queued up right next to the hotel so that they can go and see their homes, she takes a gallon of rose water with her to water her mother's grave. But she waits at the crossing for hours and hours, and nothing happens, and she ends up pouring the rose water over her face and over other people who are waiting. She pours it over them, over their heads and over their faces, over their heat — they all ran out of water a while ago. Best not to leave the house at all if you don't sprinkle your face with rose water first: it refreshes, it tones, it cauterises wounds. Seven hours she waits, seven hours she stands on her feet at the crossing; she waits to cross over, she waits by the big hotel so that she can cross over and pour some rose water over her mother's grave. She waits, together with all those who want to go visit their homes, and in the end she runs out of rose water, and she runs out of tears, and her face is all dried up — the sun and the heat and the horror dry everything up.

Rose Water:
You can put it in drinks, in the food you cook, on your bosom, and on your face.
Best not to leave the house at all if you don't sprinkle your face with rose water first to refresh you, to tone you, to cauterise your wounds.

BRANDY SOUR

***

Lemonade: The UN

In truth, only lemonade can help you bear the heat. Especially
if you make it yourself. They make a lemonade with brown
sugar and sour lemons on the island. One part brown sugar
and one part lemon juice. There are times in the afternoon
when that's the only thing that can quench her thirst.
Lemonade with brown sugar and sour lemons. Only lemonade
can help you bear the lies and the heat, really. They had, of
course, already explained the situation to them before they
got here: they had told them about the inter-communal
clashes, the Turks, the Greeks, the checkpoints – you can't
assume duties in a place, war zone or no war zone, if you are
not fully cognisant of the situation on the ground. But
nobody had warned them about the lies and the heat. And,
good-god, the heat here is something unreal. It's the kind of
heat that fills your lungs with hot air, that dries the air in your
nostrils, that dries up your face, that chops you up into pieces,
that won't let you breathe. The kind of heat that forces
everything into absolute stillness: the cicadas, the people, the
trees, the cats. A heat that feels like hell. That kind of heat.
Noons in Nicosia are dead and languid – all she can do is stay
inside the containers that were placed in the hotel yard to be
used as rooms and sleep. Sometimes, she swims in the pool
and, less often, she plays tennis with a colleague at night,
when the temperature drops enough to allow it. Beyond the
pool and the tennis court and the dining hall with the
ramshackle flooring, nothing is in use in the hotel any more,
and nothing outside it either – there's nothing to do around
this Green Line, and there's definitely nothing green about it
either. All you can do is feel thirsty and drink lemonade.

Sometimes, she takes a walk around the building, wanders around the rooms, looks at the crumbling plaster, trips over the ramshackle floors, hears the rats in the attic. Sometimes, she goes outside and walks in between the two checkpoints. Sometimes, she just looks at the building from afar, sometimes she thinks that one of these days the hotel will come crashing down, will go to smithereens, will collapse, will succumb to its own rubble. They will wake up one day only to find it dead among the ruins, killed by the war, the heat, and the lies. One day, she thinks, they'll wake up and they'll see it there, dead, and everyone will cry and they will all look at each other trying to decide who is to blame. The heat and the war and the lies will kill the building. And all the lemons in the world, all the water, all the tears won't be enough to save it.

Lemonade:
Squeeze the lemons
Brown sugar
Equal parts lemon juice and sugar
Pour into a bottle, stir until the sugar melts
Dilute with cold water
Only lemonade can help you bear the lies and the heat.

Between Two Infernos

Rezuwan Khan

Translated from the Rohingya by Hla Hla Win

HUMAN BEINGS COME INTO this world empty, naked, pure. We are born the same, and we die the same way, taking no worldly possessions with us.

One summer night, I dreamt of a garden filled with different species of flower. Among its water lilies, roses and daisies, young lovers walked, stooping under branches, whispering sweet nothings to each other. I heard a chorus of birdsong emanating from a stone birdbath bordered by daffodils and marigolds, and was overwhelmed by an aroma of happiness. Breathing it all in, I woke up suddenly, longing desperately to be there in that garden with my beloved. But as I came to my senses, I fell back into the dark pit that is life in a refugee camp.

Sandwiched between the wide, lazy Naf River and the grey Bay of Bengal, the area that's today known as Kutupalong Refugee Camp was once lush and dense with trees, even home to herds of elephants. Now the smell of verdant fields has been overcome by the open sewer that runs between the rows of tents. Women wait patiently at the water spigot. Teenagers spend their days engulfed in intense competitions of *sepak takraw*, deftly kicking a wicker ball over a net by the side of the road. Men languish in the heat, joking with each other to lessen the horror of their plight. And everyone feels trapped. I started my day, as I do every day, with the same questions:

'Am I human?'

'Why do so many obstacles stand in my soul's way?'

'Why am I trapped in a cage, like a bird?'

I am a helpless Rohingya, but I am still a human being, and the world has no right to separate or marginalise me. They have no right to lock me up or fence me into specially demarcated areas: I was not born to die before my allotted time. I deserve the same fundamental rights as everyone else. The barbed wire that surrounds the camp on all sides has dismantled my state of mind, left my life permanently baseless.

For me, being a Rohingya, I feel repression wherever I go, wherever I stay. No one wants me to live on their land, even on the land where my umbilical cord was cut. So survival becomes a daily struggle, one that is renewed afresh each morning. I am caught between the twin infernos of two countries, one where I was born and grew up, and one where I have been living as a refugee for four years. My people have been victims of a systematic genocide all their lives, subjected to decades of unimaginable abuses by Myanmar's military.

I am a survivor, but I am homeless, traumatised.

Back home in Myanmar, because of our religion and the colour of our skin, we were always treated as foreigners, segregated. We couldn't gather in groups, marry, or even travel between villages without explicit permission from the government. The hostility we faced didn't just come from the military and the authorities, it also came from extremists of other ethnicities such as the Rakhine and Burmese.

One day in August 2017, the security forces surrounded our village and set about burning it to the ground. As the bullets rang out, my mother and I managed to escape into the jungle with only the clothes on our backs. My elder brother Mohammed Zubair was not so lucky. He was handicapped and couldn't run as fast. He fell behind in the panic and to our eternal horror disappeared into the clutches of the military.

My mother and I travelled for several days over land, narrowly escaping marauding bands of Rakhine extremists by hiding in patches of reeds. We finally arrived at the water's edge and managed to board a boat across the Naf to Bangladesh.

The day I arrived in Bangladesh, I thought peace would finally enter my life. Just to pass a single quiet night, to sleep soundly, without the sound of gunshots rattling through the night would be a relief. But no, here too rifles cough louder than the rumble of thunder and bullets darken the skies like clouds of hungry locusts. Machine guns and AK47s cackle in delight, as fiery tongues run through our makeshift village, from pole to pole, post to post. Shaking, we find shelter under some broken tents. I expected this place to be a patch of heaven; but it was all a mirage, for which I have sacrificed much.

Barbed wire surrounds an overcrowded bitterness on all sides. A bamboo shelter and a ration card, with which I receive a few basic commodities, are my only possessions here. But for a family of five, these aren't enough; they won't last to the end of the month. I have no resources or income in this squalid camp, beyond that card. Eating a decent meal here is something we can only dream of.

In September 2019, the government of Bangladesh started fencing the camps in, with the aim of reducing the number of crimes being reported in the villages surrounding the camps. This fence was in addition to the checkpoints they had already set up on every road to and from the camps. By June of this year, 80 per cent of the project was completed. I say often that my people were thrown into a birdcage. But birds can't live in a cage forever, they need to fly.

The fence separates us from our basic human rights. It traps us with its coils of barbed wire in Kutupalong, the world's largest refugee camp.

Just as we faced genocide in the country of our birth, we now face a second, systematic genocide here. I've seen pictures of concentration camps, and I recognise the loops of wire.

This is the refugee life.

When I got married earlier this year, I wanted my bride to arrive from her house in a decorative carriage as is tradition; I wanted to host a party big enough for all our cherished guests. But the fence has made the road between our houses too long and our house too narrow for any carriage. Days, weeks, months go by and my younger siblings have nowhere to play. When my mother goes to the well for water, she walks an impossibly long way just to fetch it. There is no space for my younger siblings to play behind or in front of our narrow shelter.

Because of the fence, travel from one section of the camp to another is very expensive, which means that the sick and elderly have to walk long distances to seek medical attention, especially when it's only available outside the camp altogether. If I suffer a medical emergency inside the camp, there is very little hope of me being able to get proper treatment from one of the district hospitals. Covid-19 and other diseases have also risen for the Rohingya in the fenced-off camps, on account of the lack of hygiene or access to vaccines.

In March 2021, a huge fire broke out in the Balukali refugee camp, near my shelter in Kutupalong. Many people, young and old, tried to save themselves from it. Some of them managed to squeeze through small entrances or cut holes in the fence, but not everyone could escape. At least fourteen people were trapped by the barbed wire and burned to death. Overnight, 50,000 people were made homeless.

We now know that the fire was deliberately lit by gangs,

some of which are known to have links with the local authorities, who no longer want to see Rohingyas living on Bangladeshi soil. They want us to be forcibly returned to our motherland without any hope of justice for the crimes committed against us, and with the country now under military law.

Since my shack is near the fence, I feel its presence more than those who live far away from it. In the morning, as I get out of bed, I always feel like a prisoner serving a life sentence in the narrow confines of a tarpaulin shelter. On the east side of my shelter runs the main highway between Teknaf and Cox's Bazar. Despite how close I am to this road, I can't just get on it and go. If I want to leave the camp, I have to navigate through long and confusing paths to simply reach the entrance onto the highway. Some days, the local authorities deny me permission to leave – by car or even on foot – and give no reason for it. This has cut me off from anything resembling coexistence either with the host community or my relatives and friends in other camps.

Some barriers separating the Rohingyas are not made of barbed wire, but dangerous seas. Given the hardships and violence facing us inside the fence from different gangs and regional authorities, many Rohingya choose to flee the mainland altogether to Bhasan Char, a remote island in the Bay of Bengal formed out of silt only eighteen years ago. Every year, this island floods and large parts of it are washed into the roiling ocean. Still, some Rohingyas choose to flee there to escape the fence and the dangers it holds within.

During a recent mass relocation to Bhasan Char, one of my elder sisters joined the exodus with her four young daughters. Her husband had been tortured by a regional gang, who captured him at the camp's main gate as he returned home from a week of fishing off a small, coastal village. Despite having government checkpoints and guards within sight of the incident, he was dragged into a car and extorted for a large sum of money. Extortion in the camp doesn't happen *despite* the authorities' presence, it happens *because* of it, in cooperation with them.

But the worst part of the camp is the mental stress. My mind is always trying to drift back to my homeland, Arakan; but I am stuck here, utterly, with no other destination ahead of me. Instead, I often see the flames of my future, the conflagration of my fortune, trapped in this prison camp. I have worked to educate myself and to use my talents for the good of my community; but for all the energy I have right now, I fear that the isolation will one day drive me mad.

The longer I live here, the more I feel the weight of the hardships of my life bearing down on me, the more I fear that I will never break free of them. My life in this squalid camp, behind the barbed wire, is only that of one of many hundreds of thousands of Rohingya suffering every day.

I sometimes get phone calls from my old village back in Myanmar, where my once-happy home lies silent and charred. Although I feel discouraged by the fence around me, it reminds me that I am trapped first and foremost by my own government, the one that forced me to be here. It was Myanmar's government that set fire to my house. Every morning, I approach the fence from my shelter. When I stand there, I'm overcome with the fear that I may be arrested for simply coming so close to it.

But even as I stand there, alone, I try not to forget my strength, my zeal to awaken the struggle. During the two and a half decades of my life, I have felt bitterness and hatred in both Myanmar and Bangladesh. In a fraught, seething prison of people, I have, for the last four years, had to survive not just the hardships, but an abyss of ignorance within this fence.

I am starved by the scarcity of physical and intellectual sustenance inside these camps. And reflecting on my situation,

I sometimes wonder if it's better to die than to live on in this unjust world where humans are not treated equally and the wealthiest have no pity for the innocent. The right to work is denied Rohingyas like me.

Right now, a new shadow hangs over me. I pass the days and nights in fear, moving from one abandoned bamboo shelter to the next. I dare not spend too many nights in my own shelter – and when I do, I cannot sleep – for all the threats from the local gangs, promising to kidnap me for ransom money. The government might claim the fence is here to give security to the Rohingya, but in reality it is only a means to control them, and their movement.

If I'm ever set free from this prison cage, I shall rise and sprout anew like Lazarus. My shadow will grow tall and dark. I'm still a young man blessed with bundles of talent and, if free, I vow to defy all challenges, overcome all obstacles. Let my bravery and determination unlock the door that presently stands shut before me! Let me illuminate the darkness that surrounds me with the light of my education! Let me leave the insecurities and precariousness of the camp behind forever!

Mother's MacGuffin

Larissa Boehning

Translated from the German by Lyn Marven

THE RAIN STOPPED JUST after Hamburg. Ria switched off the rhythmic squeaking of the windscreen wipers and felt a keen desire to call her daughter on the car's hands-free set. Just to tell her quickly what she had suddenly remembered, a moment ago while the rain was still pattering.

Then the sky had suddenly torn apart, and that was worth a phone call too. That's how she would describe it, the way the low evening sun had broken through the clouds and set fire to the windowpanes of a house standing all alone in the middle of the fields. Pine trees lined the autobahn, towering up like a wall, perhaps even a guard of honour.

Marie would certainly stop whatever she was doing at this time of night – making spaghetti, messaging her girlfriends, drawing the perfect eyeliner in front of the mirror. But she would also say in that tone of voice that stabbed at Ria: Mama, I'm fine. You don't need to worry about me.

The former border crossing at Zarrentin couldn't be far from here. Surely there would be a sign soon, surrounded by endless pines, commemorating the fact: Here Germany was divided until 10 November 1989 at 0:32am. The Wall probably only fell in Zarrentin a few days later. She couldn't have said when. She couldn't even work out how old she had been on that journey with her mother, over to Berlin that time on the old transit road – that was the moment she had suddenly remembered just now. Had she been ten? Eleven? They had been driving over to Berlin, through the Zone as it was known in the West, for her grandfather's funeral. For the funeral of *that man*, as her mother had brusquely explained, *that man* who had somehow gone and died without Ria ever really knowing he was still alive.

In her memory, she could picture it exactly: her mother was steering with a cigarette between her index and middle fingers, there was a sheepskin on the driver's seat, with a tongue of fur hanging over the back – no headrests anywhere – and they had joined the line of traffic in front of the border crossing. Then her mother had turned round to her in the back seat and said that mysterious phrase, like she always did: wait and see what happens next.

But that's not when it started, Ria's particular weakness: she had it before then. She had always had it. In primary school she had watched the refugee girl standing apart from the others: she had come to Germany with her mother from a distant land – Iran – where there was a war going on, and Ria had wanted to heal the helpless pain, the fear in the girl's eyes. She had made friends with the girl purely for that reason, to invite her over to her house to play.

Even at that age, she should have known that she would have no luck with her mother. Quite the opposite: her mother treated the girl and Ria – her own daughter – like beggars that you give a token coin out of pity.

But still she carried on in the same vein. Right up till the end, she called her mother three times a week. Obviously hoping, somewhere in a corner of her brain, that all her quiet kindness – the constant phone calls, listening to her, never contradicting – would succeed in healing her mother from her unapproachable hardness, from that solid ring that surrounded her like the divine light radiating from an icon.

And back then, with the pale young boy from the East German border police who walked along the long column of cars, everything inside her must have kicked in: please, dear God or whoever might be in charge, put our world back in order at last, make us humans somehow able to be good to each other again, make us see that we can be friends, not a nation of enemies.

It would have been a lie to say that she had seen the boy's face in her mind's eye right now. It was rather a feeling that someone like him had been part of that moment. And Ria herself, sitting on the back seat, head bowed, waiting for the impending catastrophe: wait and see what happens next.

What? What will we see? Ria didn't say it out loud. The tongue of sheepskin lay over the back of the seat as if it was sticking out at her.

'You are my witness. In a moment you'll see them take me away.'

Take you away? Why would they do that? Who is going to take you away? In her panic, she couldn't get the words out, didn't dare ask.

'See the one at the front, the one in normal clothes? Not the soldiers over there, they are from the National People's Army. No, it'll just be the one in normal clothes who takes me away. The one wearing that impossible beige Stasi jacket. They always look like that, the Stasi men. You can tell by the way they look. Look, he's coming closer now. In a moment you'll see him take me away.'

Ria parked the car in the hotel's underground car park just after eight in the evening and the young woman on reception asked her if she had been caught up in the traffic for a long time. No, she just wasn't able to get away until early evening, was at work until late, never-ending meetings and discussions – but the young woman was already passing her ID back across the counter with that professional smile on her face that told Ria that she had taken an invitation to small talk too seriously again.

The room looked out over the Ku'damm, which she didn't remember being quite so resplendent, so full of lights and people. She quickly unpacked her suitcase, put her toiletries in the bathroom and placed the folder with the documents and her short speech on the ornate desk by the window. She was ready to call Marie and tell her – in a light-hearted, self-ironising tone of voice, of course – about this moment too. About what she was planning to do now: leave the hotel, go for a walk, stroll through the city's streets. Catch a bit of the legendary Berliner Luft, the Berlin air which was in fact nothing more than petrol-heavy, dusty smog.

Mama of mine, Marie would probably say, maybe even the next level term of endearment: *Mama my mama, you're feeling completely alone now, aren't you?*

No, she would reply, and smile. It was like a game between them. No, I've had three weeks to prepare myself for my mother's funeral, after all.

I've no idea how I would live through that, Marie would probably say.

But that's completely different, Ria would demur. And then fall silent. Don't say anything else, don't overdo it. Don't stress again how close their own relationship was.

When it's your own mother being buried, it's like the end of an era, Marie would say, or something like it, with her boundless empathy. I should have just come with you, Mama, to hell with exams.

Out of the question, Ria would have said, you're taking your exam tomorrow and that's that.

And then she would change the subject: Have you packed your bag already? Do you know what you're going to wear? Have you got a lucky mascot? Oh, and those giant energy bars which that chess grandmaster always eats?

After she had hung up, it would all sound too earnest: her words too clumsy, the distraction tactics too transparent.

Ria closed the curtain, unplugged her phone from the charger cable, grabbed her coat and bag and left her hotel room. In the lift, she looked herself in the face for a moment – the new bobbed hairstyle which made her look even more like her mother – it was just as well her mother wouldn't see that now.

Putting a spring in her step, as if she wanted to leave herself behind, she threaded her body through the hotel's revolving door, turning her collar up when she got outside. Beginning of April, still rather chilly.

From now on she would be a different woman. One who sits down without a second thought in a restaurant of her choice, orders a bottle of wine for herself – or at least an Aperol spritz – to raise a fitting toast to her mother. A final farewell to *a person that I never knew.*

She would be this different woman somehow, who would never dream of sitting down in the first empty restaurant she came across – even if it was a kebab shop glowing neon – because she couldn't bear to see the poor owner with no customers, and if she didn't he would be on the verge of having to close the shop.

She should bury that woman along with her mother. And from now on, be the woman who responded to the unhurried ministrations of a waiter with a bit of banter and a casual tip. A woman who walked past the staff in the hotel reception self-confidently as if she were here on a business trip. Who would give a eulogy at the funeral tomorrow which was perfect and her mother's colleagues and acquaintances would be proud of her.

She walked through the flickering of the lights on the Ku'damm, and left the hotel behind her. At her side, the rushing of traffic, one, two yellow double-decker buses. She passed by mannequins in shop windows wearing wedding dresses and bright spring fashions, jewellers whose windows were behind heavy shutters for the night.

She would never carry it off, being this different woman. She would forever be the person she was back at the border crossing at Zarrentin on the transit road to Berlin, when they had gone to the funeral of her mother's father, *that man*. She would always be the same girl, the same woman who didn't dare to ask any questions. Because that was the opposite of healing. Because it only opened harsh new wounds.

Wait and see what happens next.

Tell me then, what? What will we see? Who you truly are? The person you have always been?

The next morning Ria fetched herself a buttery croissant, jam, and a large white coffee in the hotel's breakfast room. She sat down at one of the tables that had been set for guests and instructed herself to enjoy this small moment of peace and quiet.

The care home in which her mother had been living was a ten-minute walk away. She finished her coffee, put her phone in her bag and set off. Ria walked in through the lobby, past all the letterboxes, and said to the care assistant who was sitting behind the reception desk, whose name – Svetlana – was on a badge on her chest, that she had an appointment with the director of the home. Svetlana looked at her for a moment as she said her surname and nodded. 'My deepest sympathies for your loss, truly.'

It sounded very honest, heartfelt somehow.

'Thank you.'

'Your mother was a wonderful woman. I have very deep

respect for her.' Svetlana put her hand to her chest, and smiled almost bashfully. Her accent also made Ria want to return her friendliness in kind, threefold, tenfold, a hundredfold.

'Thank you very much.' She couldn't bring herself to say anything more.

'It's such a shame. The funeral is tomorrow, isn't it?'

'Yes.'

'I have to work, unfortunately. I will go to her grave another day and say goodbye.'

The director came out of a meeting and distractedly, almost irritatedly, reached out a hand. She didn't even invite Ria to sit down at the imposing rosewood table in the middle of the office. She reached for the landline, pushed a single button and spoke into the receiver, saying she needed the bag from the safe immediately, as discussed. Then she apologised to Ria for having so little time – she had actually just come out of one meeting and was about to go into the next – and Ria nodded and said into the imperceptible chaos that surrounded the director, like sand strewn around the room, that someone should invent something to stop all those futile, interminable meetings, some kind of magic weapon – but at that very moment, just as the word hung pointlessly in the air, a young woman came through the side door holding a slim laptop bag in her hand. The director looked relieved.

Outside on the street again, Ria leant the bag against the back of one of the wooden benches which stood in a little circle outside the home. Names were scratched all over the green-painted slats. Ria sat down next to the bag with a last glance at the retirement village.

So these were the personal effects of her mother that she had been promised.

She had been expecting – hoping for – something with a bit more weight. Instead, it looked like there was nothing in it at all. It was nothing more than a MacGuffin. And she – Ria – had been waiting for this bag. Almost longing for it, in fact. In the belief – okay, in the hope – that she would find something truly important inside.

In one go, Ria lay the bag across her lap and opened the zip. Her watch was sticking out from under the hem of her coat sleeve. Quarter to eleven. Hopefully everything was going well for Marie. She would be in the middle of her first exam right now.

As boldly as her daughter would have done it, she lifted the cover of the laptop bag.

Two old books and an envelope. Nothing else.

She took out the yellowing envelope first. The flap was sitting in the fold. She opened it. Inside was a twenty dollar note that looked like it had been pressed flat and a visiting card – Walt E. Emerson – with an address in the district of Dahlem. From way before the postcodes changed, by the looks of it. On the back there was an old-fashioned symbol of a telephone, followed by a five-digit number. This card must be from the seventies or the early eighties at the latest, when five numbers were enough in walled-in West Berlin. She looked in the envelope again – but there was nothing else.

She ran her thumbs over the spotted pages of *For Whom the Bell Tolls* and breathed in the smell that reminded her of second-hand bookshops, or rows of boxes at the flea market that you can rummage through. That combination of old, firmly-held certainties and the ephemerality of paper. Then she reached for the other book, Heinrich Böll's *The Clown*.

There were faint pencil numbers all over the book – was that her mother's handwriting? Probably not. As she slowly flicked through the pages, she kept noticing sentences that had been annotated: *For the first time I felt more or less comfortable in this apartment; it was warm and clean, and as I hung up my coat and stood my guitar in the corner, I wondered whether*

an apartment was perhaps after all something more than a delusion.
In the margin next to this underlined sentence stood '1-292'.

Fleeing her own disappointment, she quickly put everything
back in the laptop bag, closed the zip and walked a different
way back to the hotel, through different streets. There she
stuffed the bag in the bottom drawer of the wardrobe next
to her black boots for tomorrow and closed the door. In a
café, where she treated herself to a dish from the lunch menu
with cake and espresso afterwards, she imagined for a
moment what would happen if she were to call the number
of this Walt E. Emerson, with the 030 code in front, from her
mobile phone. Right now. She had only glanced briefly at
the visiting card but had not forgotten the string of numbers.

In her imagination Mr Emerson simply picked up the call,
answering in the old-fashioned way by saying his full name,
something like that. What would she say? *Good afternoon, I just
found your telephone number in my late mother's effects, and would
like to ask you a few questions?*

She didn't actually want to know. She would accidentally
forget the bag in the hotel. Or, if not there, leave it lying on
a bench on one of the platforms at Zoologischer Garten, get
back in the car and drive home. She pictured a few platform
attendants marching up, maybe the police had been called
already, perhaps with a sniffer dog, to remove the suspicious
laptop bag. And later everyone who dealt with it would be
astounded: two old books and a dollar bill. But of course
they couldn't just dispose of the object – these absurd relics
from another time. They would have to make space for it in
the evidence room. And there it would lie, so Ria imagined,
until the end of some time or other.

She paid the bill, left a generous tip – the waitress with her
messy bun and mischievous grin had reminded her of Marie
– and left the café. She walked through Olivaer Platz, which

stretched out before her in the bright spring light. Concrete paths crossing the square, a few dogs running around, looking for the sticks and tennis balls that their owners threw across the lawns for them. She forced herself not to pick up a still-life of sandwich wrappers, bags and coffee cups that had been left lying on the grass – a few grey-black crows were picking around in the rubbish, eyeing each other with suspicion.

She would go and get her car now and drive to the cemetery where she would meet the gentleman from the undertakers who was expecting her, to discuss everything there was still left to discuss for tomorrow. She would organise everything perfectly – see it through properly to the last, people expected it of her. And then tomorrow, on the way back home, after the funeral, when it was all over and done with, once she had given her mother a fitting and decorous send-off – one she could have been proud of – then she would take the MacGuffin out of the hotel wardrobe and send it on its last journey. And with this one final memory of Berlin, she would stop being the good daughter once and for all.

It was starting to get dark by the time she walked through the gate of Zehlendorf Forest Cemetery. The pine trees, the brushwood, the earth on the trodden paths all smelled cool and musty. She noticed that she was walking faster, involuntarily. She had read on the internet, to her surprise, all the famous people buried here – Willy Brandt, Hildegard Knef, Ernst Reuter, and various former Presidents. The air was much fresher than in the city centre.

She had assumed that you needed to be a public figure to be granted your final resting place here, but the gentleman from the undertakers hadn't been shocked in the slightest, had simply given her the details of the grave, and then said she could have complete confidence in him, he knew the place well.

There he was, standing up ahead, next to the chapel, wearing a dark-grey, mid-length quilted jacket over his suit. He reached out a hand to her, as if to indicate how much distance they should keep from each other; his voice was surprisingly deep.

He appeared even more uneasy than she felt – as if he found this whole business with death distasteful somehow – and she was tempted to cover it up with small talk, to distract him from his shame, set him free.

But then words deserted her – and he also didn't seem inclined to keep any conversation going – and so they walked in silence, without saying anything at all, through the avenues, along the narrower dirt paths in the fading light towards her mother's grave.

The grave had already been prepared, the earth walls were supported by wooden boards. The undertaker kept a respectable distance, as if standing too close would come across as pushiness.

A stone tablet shone out from under the ivy that sprawled across the right-hand side of the grave.

'There's already a grave there?' she asked, turning round to the undertaker.

He took a few steps towards her, his hands crossed in front of him like a schoolboy, the left hand clasping the right wrist.

'Yes. It's a family plot, yes.'

She debated stepping onto the ivy, to pull the stems away from the stone plaque. But not in front of the undertaker. He had said it with a tone of voice that suggested he was surprised: didn't she know?

She did. She did know. It's just that nobody had told her. There was obviously only one person who could be buried here. Her mother's mother was lying somewhere in a cemetery in Münster, sharing a grave with her second husband.

Ria's mother had clearly left instructions in her will to be laid to rest next to her father. Next to *that man*. To whose funeral Ria had travelled with her mother that time. Without grasping for a second that all this, here and now, her journey back here once more, had become in this moment something like a second loop going back and forwards through time.

In the car, she plugged in her phone, connected it to the set and selected Marie's number on the display. The dialling tone sounded muffled inside the car. Her daughter let it ring and ring. Ria just got the mailbox, but she was certainly not going to tell it about the experience she had just had – this further posthumous surprise on her mother's part.

She started the engine and rolled slowly out of the car park. She resisted the urge to press redial, and instead turned the radio on. She found a station which was broadcasting news. As soon as music came on, she switched to the next one where there was an interview.

But underneath the distraction, a thought was forming. It was still out of reach, but she no longer felt like she was standing in a hollow of thick fog. Directed by the satnav, she drove back to the hotel, parked in the underground car park, and took the stairs up to the third floor. She pulled the laptop bag out of the wardrobe, took out the two books and placed them next to each other on the bedcover. Pushing against her heels, she slipped her trainers from her feet – earth from the cemetery stuck to the edges of each shoe – and sat down cross-legged at the head of the bed.

There was a dedication on the last page of the Hemingway that she had missed before: for S.P.. The numbers in the Böll next to the underlined sentences made sense too when you looked more closely. They counted how many characters there were in each one.

Ria shut the books with a snap and thought she could

smell the ancient dust billowing out from the pages. All these old stories.

Her whole life, her mother had treated her like an idiot. An idiot or just incorrigibly naïve, at any rate not worthy; she didn't deserve to be initiated into her mother's illustrious circle of mysteries. Walt E. Emerson. S.P. in the Hemingway. And now wanting to be buried next to her father. Next to *that man*, about whom she had said, after the funeral – while walking away from the grave, or in the car or somewhere else, Ria could no longer recall where – *Finally that opportunist is six foot under.*

Ria looked opportunist up in the dictionary later, after their trip through the Zone. If she remembered correctly, she had even made a note of the word in her diary.

And then the Wall fell, and her mother had stared at the images on television and said to her: Shame he's no longer with us. Such a shame. Otherwise they would get him now. Get him once and for all. And then they would see what a traitor they had nurtured in their own ranks.

Her disgust hung on every word like tar and feathers. And that was why Ria would never shake the feeling that she needed to undertake the task of making things right again, which was a superhuman feat.

Marie rang back and Ria couldn't stop questioning her about how her first exam had gone today. She probed gently, asking follow-up questions until Marie reached the point where she said: 'Honestly, nothing else happened. No drama, no blackout, no nasty teacher, nothing!'

'It's just so nice to hear your voice.'

'So is everything okay with you, Mama of mine?'

'Everything's shipshape and Bristol fashion.'

'Leave it out. Are you really okay over there in Berlin?'

'Show me the way to the next whisky bar, oh don't ask

why.' She had just heard Kurt Weill's song in a feature on the radio earlier.

'Okay, I'm starting to get a bit worried now.'

'So you should,' said Ria, 'you won't recognise me when I get back home tomorrow.'

'Goodness gracious me, whatever next.'

'Yes, better get ready because you won't know what has hit you.'

They carried on in that vein for a few more rounds, then Ria let her daughter hang up. Not without telling her to go to bed early to be fit for the next exam – and that she loved her – at which point Marie retorted: 'It's all lies. You haven't changed at all.'

She held the phone in her hand and it seemed to her that there was perhaps a brief, imperceptible shift that no one on the outside would ever comprehend or notice. Only Ria herself, just like the steps that you always have to take alone, on the ten-metre board, all the way to the edge.

The chapel in the Forest Cemetery was filling up slowly, despite the funeral having been scheduled early in the day. Ria stood at the entrance by the heavy wooden door – the funeral director opposite her – and received the handshakes and expressions of condolence from the invited guests. The idea had come to her in the middle of the night.

She clasped the hands of her mother's former colleagues – grey-haired men whose faces were tanned from overwintering in the south of Europe, who took off their leather gloves like gentlemen before extending their hands to Ria. Men who gave the impression that, if they had been wearing a homburg hat, they would have doffed it. Women dressed elegantly in black who for the most part, just as she had expected, nonchalantly looked her up and down. They would see who she really was shortly.

The funeral director gathered the flowers that had been brought and arranged them around the coffin on the steps at the front of the chapel. He waited there, to signal to her that it was about to begin.

She wanted to stay where she was, at the door. As far away as possible from the mound of flowers and the simple wooden casket in which her mother lay. With a white lily in her hand, and trembling knees, she slowly made her way towards the front, as if encountering resistance, as if the two of them were opposite magnetic poles. Her every step could be heard, leather soles on smooth stone; then finally the organ came in with an airy, bright note.

She walked along the aisle with the mourners' eyes upon her, and she could feel the sympathy, the well wishes and a hint of condescension. She could see what they were thinking: a daughter who had never attained her mother's stature.

The funeral director stepped aside, as if making way for the white lily that she was holding in front of her. It made her knees go even weaker. Not even halfway to the coffin.

On no account is anyone to lay a socialist-red carnation on my grave, or a white lily for that matter. Those were her mother's instructions in a letter to the undertakers. So was the piece that the organist was playing right now – Chopin's Nocturne op. 9, no. 2. So was the plot next to her father's grave – next to *that man*. She was always allowed to surprise others like that. But no one surprised her.

Ria was getting slower, she walked through the organ's chords, through the almost cheerful nocturne. Came to a halt next to her mother's coffin.

'After considerable deliberation, I decided on this lily,' she said softly, so softly that no one would hear beneath the music. There they lay, the open petals, the long stems on the wood.

She breathed in the heavy, almost intoxicating scent, and

stood there with her back to the mourners until Chopin's light-hearted piece had faded away in the air.

As she turned around, a man slipped through the entrance door and sat down, energetically for his age – rather messy grey hair standing on end – in the last row, where he smiled an apology to her. So charmingly, she almost returned his smile out of reflex.

At the pulpit, she unfolded the piece of paper that she had taken out of the little desk in the hotel in the middle of the night. Her window had been ajar and on the Ku'damm outside it was perfectly still, no cars, no double-decker buses.

She had seen before her very eyes, with complete clarity, what she would say today, now, during the funeral, what she was just about to say, right now.

Carefully she smoothed out the creases in the paper with her hand.

No address to the mourners, no pretence at niceties. Just: Dear Mama. Or should I say: Dear woman that I never knew, who I so dearly wished had been my mother…

The man with the messy hair had approached her. Afterwards. Only now, when she had been in the car for some time, on the motorway, speeding away from the Forest Cemetery, did she try to put everything that had happened into some meaningful order – the old man with the messy hair had approached as she was standing by the grave. He had stood there with her for a moment and made no moves to pick up the shovel with the earth or throw some flowers into the depths. Her attention was drawn to his highly polished, probably hand-stitched shoes, in contrast to his unruly mop of hair.

'It's not easy to find the right words,' he said at some point. 'But you didn't beat about the bush there.' Was that approval in his voice?

'How did you know my mother?'

'I didn't know her. I knew her father, the old gentleman who is lying here next to her.'

He gave her a sidelong smile, as if he was hoping for something like a pardon from her.

'And how did you know my grandfather, whom I never knew either?'

'Mutual cooperation, we had a good working relationship.'

She left it hanging. Slowly it sank onto firm ground.

'I think I can guess,' Ria had said.

'I thought so. You already know, don't you.'

'If I'm being completely honest – I don't want to have anything more to do with all that.'

'There are some walls that we will never tear down,' the old man had said and extended his hand to say goodbye. She had grasped it and marvelled at how firm and strong his grip was. And then he had turned around and walked away from the grave, along the trodden earth path, and at the next corner he strode off through the dark pine forest, as if he knew the way.

She had waited, expecting to feel an impulse to run after him, to question him after all, to try to understand. Or, if nothing else, to contradict him – to say there are no walls that can't be torn down! That we can always do it, if only we wanted to. That conflict can be healed, if we would only talk to each other.

Nothing. She stood there, by her mother's grave, and no longer felt any desire to understand these incomprehensible things. To heal this distance. To make anything right.

She placed both hands firmly on the steering wheel and stretched her back in the driver's seat. Just fifty kilometres to Hamburg and a blazing blue sky over the fields of stubble. She had only seen a sign that marked the new federal-state border, but no reminder of the border crossing at Zarrentin. But maybe she had just missed it.

Soon, when she got home, she would tell Marie about everything. Make afternoon coffee for them both, sit down at the kitchen table, and tell her everything. She would look her daughter in the eyes and wouldn't leave a single bit out. Even though it was still a mystery to Ria herself.

About the Editors

Will Forrester is Translation and International Manager at English PEN. He has worked with Commonwealth Writers, in the visual arts in Kuala Lumpur, and with Untold on *My Pen Is the Wing of a Bird: New Fiction by Afghan Women*. He is an editor at *Review 31,* and his writing has appeared in *The Guardian, Los Angeles Review of Books, London Magazine, and elsewhere.*

Sarah Cleave is Editor of *Banthology: Stories from Unwanted Nations* and *Europa28: Writing by Women on the Future of Europe.* She is Publishing Manager at Comma Press and Lecturer at Manchester Metropolitan University.

About the Authors

Born in Berlin in 1971, **Larissa Boehning** is a writer, graphic designer and lecturer. Her works include *Nichts davon stimmt, aber alles ist wahr* and *Lichte Stoffe* (Eichborn, 2007), which was longlisted for the German Book Prize and recipient of the Mara Cassens Prize for best debut novel in 2007. Her debut short story collection, *Swallow Summer*, translated by Lyn Marven, was published in English by Comma Press, and shortlisted for the 2017 Warwick Prize for Women in Translation.

Zahra El Hasnaoui Ahmed was born in Aaiún, the old capital of Spanish Sahara. She studied languages in Madrid and London and works as a teacher. She is a member of the Saharawi Friendship Generation and author of *The Silence of the Clouds.*

Maya Abu Al-Hayyat is the director of the Palestine Writing Workshop, an institution that seeks to encourage reading in Palestinian communities through creative writing projects and storytelling with children and teachers. She has published four collections of poetry, four novels, and numerous children's stories, including *The Blue Pool of Questions*. She contributed to and wrote a foreword for *A Bird Is Not a Stone: An Anthology of Contemporary Palestinian Poetry*, and edited *The Book of Ramallah* (Comma Press, 2021). Her work has appeared in the *Los Angeles Review of Books, Cordite Poetry Review, The Guardian,* and *Literary Hub*. She lives in Jerusalem and works in Ramallah.

Muyesser Abdul'ehed (pen name: Hendan) is a poet, writer and educator. A native of Ghulja in the north of East Turkistan, she completed a medical degree at Beijing University, followed by a master's in University of Malaya. After relocating to Turkey in 2013, she resolved to focus on writing and teaching the Uyghur language. Her debut novel, *Kheyr-khosh, quyash* ('Farewell, Sun') is the first work of fiction to focus on the internment camps in East Turkistan.

Rezuwan Khan is a Rohingya poet, folklorist and community-based private teacher living in the Kutupalong Rohingya refugee camp, in Cox's Bazar, Bangladesh. He is also the author of *Rohingya Folktales,* a book and website dedicated to capturing the stories of the Rohingya people across Arakan.

Paulo Scott was born in 1966 in Porto Alegre, in southern Brazil, and grew up in a working-class neighbourhood. At university, he was an active member of the student political movement and was also involved in Brazil's re-democratisation process. For fourteen years he taught law at university in Porto Alegre. He has now published six books of fiction and seven of poetry, as well as one graphic novel. He has lived in London, Rio de Janeiro and Garopaba, and moved to São Paulo in 2019 to focus on writing full-time.

Kyung-Sook Shin is one of South Korea's most widely read and acclaimed novelists. She has been awarded the Man Asian Literary Prize, the Manhae Grand Prize for Literature, the Dong-in Literature Prize, the Yi Sang Literary Prize, and many others, including France's Prix de l'Inaperçu. Shin is the author of multiple books, including *The Girl Who Wrote Loneliness, I'll Be Right There, The Court Dancer, Violets,* and the *New York Times*-bestselling *Please Look After Mom,* which has been published in over forty countries.

Geetanjali Shree was born in Mainpuri, India, in 1957. She is the author of three novels and several story collections, and her work has been translated into English, French, German, Serbian and Korean. Her work has received a number of awards, including the 2022 International Booker Prize for *Tomb of Sand* (Tilted Axis, 2021), translated by Daisy Rockwell. Shree currently lives in New Dehli.

Constantia Soteriou has written three novels. *Aishe Goes on Vacation* and *Voices Made of Soil* were shortlisted for the Greek and Cypriot National Book Awards. Her short story, 'Death Customs', translated into English by Lina Protopapa, was the winner of the 2019 Commonwealth Short Story Prize. *Bitter Country*, her most recent book, revolves around the final moments of the mother of an eighteen-year-old man who went missing in the 1974 coup d'état.

Krisztina Tóth is one of Hungary's most highly acclaimed poets and writers. She has published many volumes of poetry, several collections of short stories and children's books, and a novel, *Aquarium,* which was shortlisted for the German Internationaler Literaturpreis in 2015. Her short story collection *Pixel*, translated by Owen Good, was published in English by Seagull Books.

Juan Pablo Villalobos was born in Guadalajara, Mexico, in 1973. He has written articles for many international publications, short stories and six novels, including *Down the Rabbit Hole*, which was translated into twenty languages and shortlisted for the Guardian First Book Award, *Quesadillas, I'll Sell You a Dog, I Don't Expect Anyone to Believe Me* and *The Invasion of the Spirit People* (all published by And Other Stories). He lives in Barcelona, Spain, with his wife and their two sons, where he teaches literature and creative writing.

About the Translators

Munawwar Abdulla is the co-founder of the Tarim Network, a scientist, and a passionate writer and Uyghur literary translator. She also works on initiatives like the Uyghur Collective.

Daniel Hahn is a writer, editor and translator with sixty-something books to his name. His work has won him the Independent Foreign Fiction Prize, the Blue Peter Book Award and the International Dublin Literary Award, and he has been shortlisted for the Man Booker International Prize, among others.

Rosalind Harvey is a Fellow of the Royal Society of Literature, has taught translation at the universities of Bristol and Warwick, and is a founding member of the Emerging Translators Association.

Anton Hur is a Korean translator and writer. He's won a PEN Translates award, a PEN/Heim grant, and was double-longlisted and shortlisted for the 2022 International Booker Prize. He lives in Seoul.

Lyn Marven is Reader in Contemporary German Literature and Translation at the University of Liverpool and a translator of contemporary German literature. Her translations include Maike Wetzel's short story collection *Long Days* (Comma Press, 2008) and Larissa Boehning's *Swallow Summer*, which was shortlisted for the 2017 Warwick Prize for Women in Translation.

Dorothy Odartey-Wellington is the author of *Contemporary Spanish Fiction: Generation X* (2008) and the editor of the collection of essays *Trans-Afrohispanismos: Puentes culturales críticos entre África, Latinoamérica y España* (2018). She has also published several journal articles and book chapters on Afro-Hispanic literatures and cultures from Equatorial Guinea and Western Sahara. Her current research explores the representations of Saharawi identity in exile.

Lina Protopapa is a translator based in Nicosia, Cyprus. Her translation of Constantia Soteriou's 'Death Customs' from the Greek won the 2019 Commonwealth Short Story Prize, while her translation of Nikolas Kyriakou's 'The Debt' was shortlisted for the same prize in 2020.

Daisy Rockwell is a painter, writer and translator living in Vermont, US. She has translated a number of classic works of Hindi and Urdu literature, including *A Gujarat Here, a Gujarat There* by Krishna Sobti (Penguin, 2019) and *Tomb of Sand* (Tilted Axis, 2021) by Geetanjali Shree, winner of the 2022 International Booker Prize.

Yasmine Seale is a writer and translator living in Paris. Her essays, poetry, visual art, and translations from Arabic and French have appeared widely. She is the author, with Robin Moger, of *Agitated Air: Poems after Ibn Arabi* (Tenement Press, 2022). Other work includes *Aladdin: a New Translation* (2018) and *The Annotated Arabian Nights* (2021), both out from W. W. Norton.

Peter Sherwood is a freelance translator based in London. With his wife Julia Sherwood, he has translated from the Slovak novels by Peter Krištúfek and Ján Johanides, among others. Peter taught Hungarian language and culture at the University of London and the University of North Carolina

– Chapel Hill. His translations from Hungarian include works by Miklós Vámos, Noémi Szécsi, Béla Hamvas, János Pilinszky and Ádám Bodor.

Hla Hla Win is a Rohingya writer and teacher, living in in the Kutupalong Rohingya refugee camp, in Cox's Bazar, Bangladesh with her husband and daughter.

Refugee Tales: Volume I

978-1-91097-423-0 • £9.99

Featuring: Patience Agbabi, Jade Amoli-Jackson, Chris Cleave, Stephen Collis, Inua Ellams, Abdulrazak Gurnah, David Herd, Marina Lewycka, Avaes Mohammad, Hubert Moore, Ali Smith, Dragan Todorovic, Carol Watts & Michael Zand

Refugee Tales: Volume II

978-1-91097-430-8 • £9.99

Featuring Caroline Bergvall, Josh Cohen, Ian Duhig, Rachel Holmes, Jackie Kay, Olivia Laing, Helen Macdonald, Neel Mukherjee, Alex Preston, Kamila Shamsie & Marina Warner

Refugee Tales: Volume III

978-1-91269-711-3 • £9.99

Featuring Monica Ali, Lisa Appignanesi, David Constantine, Bernardine Evaristo, Patrick Gale, Abdulrazak Gurnah, David Herd, Emma Parsons, Ian Sansom, Jonathan Skinner, Gillian Slovo, Lytton Smith, Roma Tearne & Jonathan Wittenberg

Refugee Tales: Volume IV

978-1-91269-748-9 • £9.99

Featuring Shami Chakrabarti, Kyon Ferril, Christy Lefteri, Robert Macfarlane, Khodadad Mohammadi, Dina Nayeri, Amy Sackville, Philippe Sands, Rachel Seiffert, Natalia Sierra, Bidisha SK Mamata, Simon Smith & Maurizio Veglio

The American Way

Edited by Orsola Casagrande & Ra Page

Following the US's bungled withdrawal from Afghanistan, and the scenes of chaos at Kabul Airport, we could be forgiven for thinking we're experiencing an 'end of empire' moment, that the US is entering a new, less belligerent era in its foreign policy, and that its tenure as self-appointed 'global policeman' is coming to an end.

Before we get our hopes up though, it's wise to remember exactly what this policeman has done, for the world, and ask whether it's likely to change its behaviour after any one setback. After 75 years of war, occupation, and political interference, the US military-industrial complex doesn't seem to know how to stop.

This anthology explores the human cost of these many interventions onto foreign soil, with stories by writers from that soil – covering everything from torture in Abu Ghraib, to coups and counterrevolutionary wars in Latin America, to all-out invasions in the Middle and Far East. Alongside testimonies from expert historians and ground-breaking journalists, these stories present a history that too many of us in the West simply pretend never happened.

Featuring Talal Abu Shawish, Gabriel Ángel, Gioconda Belli, Gianfranco Bettin, Najwa Bin Shatwan, Hassan Blasim, Paige Cooper, Ahmel Echevarría Peré, Hüseyin Karabey, Wilfredo Mármol Amaya, Lina Meruane, Lidudumalingani, Fiston Mwanza Mujila, Payam Nasser, Fariba Nawa, Jacob Ross, Bina Shah, Kim Thúy & Carol Zardetto

ISBN: 978-1-91269-739-7
£14.99

Europa28

Edited by Sarah Cleave & Sophie Hughes

'To be European,' writes Leïla Slimani, 'is to believe that we are, at once, diverse and united, that the Other is different but equal.' Despite these high ideals, however, there is a growing sense that Europe needs to be fixed, or at the least seriously rethought. The clamour of rising nationalism – alongside widespread feelings of disenfranchisement – needs to be addressed if the dreams of social cohesion, European integration, perhaps even democracy are to be preserved.

This anthology brings together 28 acclaimed women writers, artists, scientists and entrepreneurs from across the continent to offer new perspectives on the future of Europe, and how it might be rebuilt. Featuring essays, fictions and short plays, Europa28 asks what it means to be European today and demonstrates – with clarity and often humour – how women really do see things differently.

Featuring Asja Bakić, Zsófia Bán, Annelies Beck, Silvia Bencivelli, Hilary Cottam, Lisa Dwan, Yvonne Hofstetter, Nora Ikstena, Maarja Kangro, Kapka Kassabova, Sofia Kouvelaki, Carine Krecké, Caroline Muscat, Nora Nadjarian, Ioana Nicolaie, Bronka Nowicka, Tereza Nvotová, Ana Pessoa, Edurne Portela, Julya Rabinowich, Karolina Ramqvist, Apolena Rychlíková, Renata Salecl, Leïla Slimani, Janne Teller, Saara Turunen, Žydrūnė Vitaitė & Gloria Wekker

ISBN: 978-1-91269-729-8
£12.99